Diaspora City

Diaspora City

The London New Writing Anthology

Introduction by
Nick McDowell

A

ARCADIA BOOKS
LONDON

Arcadia Books Ltd
15–16 Nassau Street
London W1W 7AB
www.arcadiabooks.co.uk

First published in the United Kingdom 2003
Reprinted 2004

A catalogue record for this book is available from the British Library.

ISBN 1-900850-75-3

Typeset in Scala by Northern Phototypesetting Co. Ltd, Bolton
Printed in the United Kingdom by J W Arrowsmith Ltd, Bristol

Arcadia Books distributors are as follows:

in the UK and elsewhere in Europe:
Turnaround Publishers Services
Unit 3, Olympia Trading Estate
Coburg Road
London N22 6TZ

in the US and Canada:
Independent Publishers Group
814 N. Franklin Street
Chicago, IL 60610

in Australia:
Tower Books
PO Box 213
Brookvale, NSW 2100

in New Zealand:
Addenda
Box 78224
Grey Lynn
Auckland

in South Africa:
Quartet Sales and Marketing
PO Box 1218
Northcliffe
Johannesburg 2115

Arcadia Books: *Sunday Times* Small Publisher of the Year 2002/03

Contents

Introduction

As readers, we know two Londons. One is composed of streets, parks and people, the other is made up by its writers – Chaucer, Pepys, Dickens, Martin Amis, Peter Ackroyd, Hanan al-Shaykh or Zadie Smith. The capital city of thirty-three boroughs and eight million citizens, is also a palimpsest of thousands of stories – think of Naipaul's *Half a Life*, Maggie Gee's *The White Family*, Bernardine Evaristo's *The Emperor's Babe* or Rose Tremain's *Restoration*.

This is the fifth anthology of new writing to result from the biennial London New Writing Competition and the first to be produced in partnership with Arcadia Books, this year's *Sunday Times* Small Publisher of the Year. As in previous years, commissioned work from established writers – John Berger, Maggie Gee, Toby Litt, Ben Okri, Iain Sinclair and A. Sivanandan, – sits alongside stories from outstanding new voices. The stories collected in this volume reflect a London in which hundreds of cultures co-exist, enrich and challenge each other. These fictions encourage us to revisit our ideas of what it means to be foreign or assimilated, to remain other or come together.

The theme of diaspora was chosen to encourage entries from and about Londoners with roots and heritage in countries and cultures across the world. As part of the competition, workshops all over the capital – by Writers Inc., Disability Arts Forum, Exiled Writers Ink!, Centerprise, Spread the Word and Eastside Arts – offered technical help to writers at the start of their careers. Almost three hundred entries were reduced to a shortlist by Julian Keeling, Ferdinand Dennis and Catherine Johnson. Thank you to these people and organizations for their work. The winning story, *The River Underground* by Richard Tromans, together with the eight other stories included in the anthology, were chosen by publishers Gary Pulsifer and Daniela de Groote of Arcadia Books and Rosemaire Hudson of BlackAmber (who was an invaluable consultant throughout the project). Many congratulations to the nine writers published for the first time in this anthology.

As I write, a campaign is underway to resuscitate the ailing short story and coax it back to artistic and commercial prominence. The genre appears to have lost favour with British publishers and readers alike, while in the Americas and mainland Europe it remains enduringly popular. In the last year, only twenty short story collections were released by British mainstream publishers (and more than half were by writers from abroad).

Yet, according to research conducted by *Mslexia* magazine, more people in England are writing short stories than any other literary form. The short story is the genre most frequently chosen by new and emerging writers in search of their voices. About half of the Granta *Best of Young British Novelists 2003* have published collections of stories, many as a stepping stone to writing novels. It is painful to imagine a literary culture stripped of the short stories of Raymond Carver, Shena Mackay, Hanif Kureishi, Helen Simpson, Ian McEwan, Jackie Kay or Will Self (the full list gets very long indeed).

The work gathered here celebrates London's diversity, its strangeness and its enduring potency as a setting for fiction. Let's hope it will remind readers that short stories, at their brief and punchy best, can sate the appetite for fiction with elegance and brevity. Please read them. And tell your friends to read them.

Nick McDowell
Head of Literature
London Arts
January 2003

Rare Books and Manuscripts

Toby Litt

His name came as a gift to her.

She was walking down the stairs into the cafeteria; he was sitting at a table directly below them. His locker key was lying beside his cup and saucer, face up. She kept moving so as not to be in any way conspicuous. The number was easily readable, instantly memorable: 33. She almost fell down the second flight.

The cafeteria in the new British Library building, despite being new, and despite being in the British Library, was like any works cafeteria – tables too close together, conversations between people who meet too often. The talk here was a different kind of shop – "It's not that I disagree with Jaspers . . ." or "You know, CPE's the really interesting one" – but shop all the same.

It had been so easy, after all those weeks of adoring speculation – it had been so easy for her to stroll shakily down to the lower ground floor, look in the battered folder where readers signed out locker keys, find the number 33 and finally discover her true love's name and, as a bonus, his reader's card number. She memorized both: Heinz Feldman, 126153FEL. And then, when discreetly hidden in a cubicle in the women's loos, she wrote them down on the ludicrous pretence she might forget them.

Heinz – not the name she'd fantasized for him, though she'd overheard him and his friends often enough – in the canteen, in the queue for the cloakroom – to know he was German. Heinz – not a particularly romantic name, reminding her more of baked beans than of its blue-eyed owner.

Yet he remained as delectably lovely as when first she'd spotted him. On that day, one of the earliest of the winter term, he had arrived and sat down at the desk immediately facing her own. Never since had she dared sit so close, and as he always tried to get the same desk there was no danger of their coinciding by chance.

Everything about him – everything, at least, that she could see – was long: face, fingers, hair. He looked – the word was aristocratic.

She listened that first day to his breathing, which was quiet and slow. She was convinced that she would smell him.

When, for half an hour or so, she saw that he was away from his desk, she worked up courage to have a passing look at the books upon it. There were five biographies of Schubert. She fell in love.

From then on, she watched him. He was delectable. He always looked so existentially anguished, especially when bored; his long fingers raking up hanks of his thick blonde hair. He was lost, without the energy even to disguise the fact.

All of which gave her a thrilling desire to comfort him, to offer him the paltry solace of her flesh, the forgetfulness of the clasp and clutch, the brief self-absence – or total self-presence – of orgasm.

She did not allow herself to go that far in thought. But it was what she meant when at night she hugged herself close – and the idea of Heinz even closer.

She felt herself to be, in comparison, a terribly inconsequential thing, a little white bubble, a blob of blubber, a blubble.

What gave definition to Heinz were his long straight lines, and she had none of those.

Them together, say at the altar, would make a sentence comprised of a capital letter I and a full stop.

It did not escape her notice, or fail to contribute to her hopes, that such a sentence was – despite its somewhat ludicrous appearance – grammatically comprehensible.

That famous day she left early, taking his name home with her like a wallet of developed but unlooked-at photographs. All afternoon she had deferred her own pleasure, denying herself the full ecstasy of contemplating it, him, Heinz, uninterruptedly.

The bus journey over, she lay back on her single bed and thought about Heinz. He was more hers now than he'd ever been before.

When from now on she looked at him, across the desks, between the bad-haircut academic heads, she would know she had something on him. It was a form of intimacy, although hopeless.

That evening more than most, even when brushing her teeth, she avoided looking at herself too closely in the bathroom mirror. She did not want to inflict that humiliation upon herself.

It was not until she was back at the British Library the next day with one of their book-ordering terminals in front of her that she realized what she could now do: by entering Heinz's reader number instead of her own, she could order up books as if she were him – she could order up books for him.

The maximum total order was twelve in a day. It was still early that Tuesday: he wouldn't have ordered that many books yet. Plus, the Schubert biographies were always fairly constant on his desk; he never seemed to have more than four or five up at a time.

She went to have a coffee in the cafeteria whilst she deciding which book she would have ordered for him if she were going to, which of course she wasn't.

Part of the game she was playing with herself depended upon her believing she would only ever order one book for him, and so the book – whatever it was – had to be just the right one.

She couldn't decide without consulting the catalogue. And so, at a terminal in the Rare Books and Manuscripts room, far away from where she usually worked in Humanities One, she looked up title after possible title. She considered –

You don't know me, but –
Winfield, George
1978
X.435/713

She horrified herself with the thought of ordering –

I know you really love me, a psychiatrist's journal of erotomania, stalking and obsessive love
Orien, Doreen
1997
YA.1998.b.640

But in the end, after considering variations upon Hello, she settled for –

Bonjour tristesse. Roman.
Sagan, Françoise, pseud. [i.e. Françoise Quoirez]
1955
12513.tt.44.

Before placing the order, she made sure she had a desk in Humanities One positioned close to the Issue Desk. That way, when Heinz came up to collect the book, she would be on hand to see his reaction. Then she went back to the far corner of Rare Books and Manuscripts and tremblingly typed Heinz' reader number into the oblong box. She was convinced an alarm would go off – that she'd be stopped, exposed, laughed at, banned. But the order was accepted as quietly as the tens of thousands of others placed every day. This one was different, however: this one was the first message exchanged in what was destined to be (or so she fantasized) one of the great love stories of our time.

She didn't leave her seat for the next four hours. Of course, she hadn't been daring or stalkerish enough to enter his desk number when she'd ordered the book. (She'd known his desk number by heart since the first day she'd seen him; he always sat at the same – 1818.) This meant that Heinz wouldn't receive the usual notification of a book's having arrived – the words *Please contact Issue Desk* lighting up in green letters in front and to the right of him. Whilst waiting, she stared at the order notification square on her own desk. How often the illumination of that little square, announcing new books, had been the highlight of her day, and now there was this.

Finally, he stood up and walked towards the Issue Desk. It was a quiet afternoon, and there was no queue. She went rigid with horror as the librarian took Heinz' name and went off back into the stacks to look for his book – actually, books. Why had she done it? It was madness.

For one terrible moment it seemed that a very pretty young woman complaining to another librarian about something or other would obscure both the sight and sound of Heinz' reaction. But the young woman turned away in silent disgust just before the librarian returned.

In his hand she saw Sagan's book, or what she thought was Sagan's book. She'd ordered the first edition, in French. *Bonjour tristesse* was a small, darkish blue hardback with oblong gold lettering on the spine.

Heinz' reaction was delightfully what she had anticipated. He held the book in his hand – he touched it! – and looked at it in puzzlement. "But I didn't order this," he said, somewhat arrogantly. She watched to make sure he took in the title. He did, she was sure. "What would I want with this?" he asked.

"You don't want it, then?" the librarian said.

"I'm afraid that I don't," Heinz replied.

"You're not missing any other books, are you?" said the librarian, treating this reader with unusual respect.

"No," said Heinz, "I quite definitely ordered only one."

"Sorry," said the librarian, and put the Sagan on the trolley that would return it to the bookstacks in the basement.

The following day, at a far terminal in Rare Books and Manuscripts, she bravely ordered the same copy of *Bonjour tristesse* for herself.

When it arrived, she touched it breathlessly. He had held it, if only for a moment, in those long-fingered hands of his; the thought was almost unbearable. Pretending to look closely at some detail in the binding, she took a deep sniff. The sweet smell of that first encounter was confirmed. Even if it wasn't his actual scent, he'd smell of libraries, wouldn't he?

Never had she dreamt of ordering one of his finished-with Schubert biographies. They'd all had to be bought at Waterstone's, out of her measly grant.

She would lie on her bed, immersing herself in the exact same words he had recently read and in her tape of *Death and the Maiden.*

Secretly, she thought of herself as Schubert – twice as loveable as he was unloved.

Her feelings towards Schubert were so strong that she wanted to fight her way back through time and shout at him, in German, *You are loved!*

A similar instinct gave her the idea for her second book order, which she placed the following day –

You are now entering the human heart
Frame, Janet
1984
X.958/25269

This time, in her most daring move yet, when he went up to collect his books, she went and joined the queue two places behind him.

To her astonishment, he didn't seem to notice the extra one among his pile. He took the four books back to his desk without checking the titles; something – or someone – must be on his mind; someone not Schubert.

She gave up on the idea of being close by to observe his reaction when he read the title. It was just too dangerous.

Instead, she went back and sat down at her usual place – and waited for him to come up and return the book.

After an hour, it was clear that he either still hadn't noticed the title or was delaying returning the book until he had some others to collect.

After another half hour, she had become too impatient to wait. She went speciously to check a reference work at Heinz' end of Humanities One – an area of sacredness she hardly dared ever profane.

Her emotions on seeing him actually reading the Janet Frame stories, and with a half-smile upon his face, can hardly be described.

He had accepted her gift – even though he must have supposed it came from an overworked librarian or a fuddled computer.

As she had ordered the book up solely for its title, she had no idea what might be making him smile.

She felt stupid and wished she'd done her research better beforehand. She resolved never to make the same mistake again. From now on she would read every word of every book she ordered for Heinz. (And, this one having been such a success, she could hardly not order him any more.)

Over the next three days, she spent much of her time researching which books to send him.

As the Janet Frame had been such a success, she considered sending him some more of her writings. That seemed a bit too obvious, though. She stuck to the meaning in the titles. Her next three choices were –

You are wanted. [A broadcast address]
Waterhouse, Eric Strickland
1939
4480.ee.9

You Are the One
Ruck, afterwards Onions, Amy Roberta
1946
NN.35799

You are – going to build a cake factory
Crewe, Bob
1987
Cup.936/169

The latter would at least show him that his mysterious book-sender (for surely now he must have worked that out) had a sense of humour.

Almost immediately she had abandoned her resolution and had given up reading these books in their entirety; they were so bad she was sure Heinz would only glance at them.

Sunday interfered with her plans, but by Monday she had built up enough courage to make the ultimate declaration –

I love you, I love you, I love you
Bemelmans, Ludwig
1943
12332.eee.19.

She particularly liked that eee in the shelfmark – it sort of summed up how she felt.

During all this time, her own proper research had been a little neglected. This game was so much more fun.

After declaring herself, she remembered that she had a meeting at the end of the week with her PhD supervisor. For the next few days she decided to send Heinz –

Isn't it romantic?
Korbel, Kathleen
1992
H.92/2509

Isn't it wonderful? A history of magic and mystery . . . With numerous illustrations by Phil May, etc.

L.P. Bertram, Charles, pseud. [i.e. James Bassett.]
1896
7915.dd.22

Isn't it odd?
Merrywhistle, Marmaduke, pseud.
1822
N.85

That would keep her, and him, going.

She turned her attention back to Henry James' unfinished novels. She ordered some books she needed to check. She went and hid herself out of temptation's way in a far corner of Rare Books and Manuscripts. In the first batch of James that she ordered, a stray book appeared by mistake –

Rand, Ann and Rand (Paul) writer for children
I Know a Lot of Things. [An illustrated children's book.]
1957
12839.b.17

Made suspicious by her own activities, still she dismissed it as result of a glitchy computer. But when the following title appeared an hour or so later –

About you and me
Thomas, M.A.
1975
YA.1988.a.20722

– she knew that someone was on to her.

She tried to think back. Whenever she could, she got herself a locker instead of using the queuey cloakroom; she often had coffee in the cafeteria; she no doubt had sat there, even after finding out Heinz' name in this way, with her locker key face up beside her. But the thought that anyone would be interested enough in her to do the same thing just hadn't occurred.

She looked around the vast L-shaped reading room. No-one met her eye. Yet surely he would want to be close, so as to check her reaction. (He – he or she.) The idea that someone might want to sit where they could see her! It was almost unimaginable; it had certainly never happened before.

She went and sat at one of the book-ordering terminals. She could semi-sense being watched, but she thought it was probably hypersensitivity brought on by the weirdness of this situation. She couldn't concentrate, and repeatedly fumbled her typing.

Feeling unnerved, she left the library and did not return for several days. Receiving the two books had made her consider the effect her book orders might have made upon Heinz. She reassured herself with the thought that he had seemed more amused than scared. Her by-proxy messages to him had been witty and feminine; the two she'd received had been vaguely threatening.

When she returned to the library, several book orders she hadn't made were awaiting her.

Now
1977
YK.1994.a.10801

Baby!
Asquith, Ros
1988
YV.1988.a.1514

Coffee, adapted from the text written by Joseph Philippe, illustrated by Louis Joos
1976
X.329/10506.Woolwich

Coffee, now, baby!

This was terrible. She could no longer go anywhere near the cafeteria for fear of appearing to encourage her secret admirer to join her, or worse.

That lunch break she had to go down the road to a greasy spoon near Kings Cross.

As she ate her scrambled eggs on toast, she wondered whether she should ask one of the librarians if this had happened to anyone else before.

But there was always the possibility that Heinz had told them about his message books. That would make her a suspect in his case, and she might be forced to confront him. The idea was unbearable.

The only other option was the one she took: on returning to the library she went and looked up a book with the necessary title – then ordered it for herself. On the basis that her admirer was watching her closer than she had ever dared watch Heinz, she assumed that – as long as she spent enough time away from it – he would read the titles of any books left upon her desk.

The book she ordered was –

Leave me alone
Karp, David
1957
NNN.10983

She kept it uppermost on her pile for the next few hours, at the end of which she received –

Apologies et rétractions. Manuscrits inédits publiés avec une introduction et des notes par François Secret
1972
X.520/7456

(She was amused by the name François Secret, and immediately nicknamed her admirer that.) Shortly followed by –

Can we talk? the power and influence of talk shows
Scott, Gini Graham
1996
YC.1996.a.4803

Only now did she begin truly to appreciate the resources of the library. For every thing she wanted to say, there seemed to have been a book written with that exact title. What she wanted to say this time was very simple –

No way
ed David, Philip J. and David Park
1987
YH.1987.b.663

To which François Secret replied –

Please [A picture book for children]
Ackley, Edith Flack and Ackley, Telka
1943
12821.a.37

This second correspondence had completely put her off sending any further messages of love to Heinz. She knew now, sort of, how she would have appeared to him. Appeared, that is, in her invisibility.

She had no idea what François Secret looked like, but she automatically assumed the worst. To her shame, she realized that had Heinz made the same assumption in her own case, he would have been pretty close to the hideous truth.

There had been a moment, but only a very short and deluded one, during which she had believed that the book-messages were coming to her from Heinz himself. Somehow, she fantasized, he has discovered who I am, he has copied me, he reciprocates, he loves me.

Ultimately, though, she knew that her Heinz-radar was so highly-sensitive that he couldn't come within a hundred yards of her without her knowing it. Plus the fact that there was no way he would ever find her attractive. Not in this particularly shitty version of the universe, anyway. She had faced the horror of herself in the bathroom mirror too many times, too honestly – or so she thought – for her to have any long-lasting illusions about that.

The whole attraction of her book-message correspondence with Heinz had been that it was completely one-sided.

Quietly – no, silently – she had sent him her anonymous love. Nothing had been expected in return. His half-smile at Janet Frame had been more than she had ever hoped. With her admirer, though, the proposal had been instantaneous. He wanted to meet. That, for him, was the whole point of the game.

For the next few days, he repeatedly sent her –

Please [A picture book for children]
Ackley, Edith Flack and Ackley, Telka
1943
12821.a.37

– and she repeatedly returned it to the bookstacks. The librarians were beginning to look at her rather weirdly.

Finally she decided that she would have to confront François Secret, whoever he was. This wasn't a brave move as such; she was acting out of fear that if she didn't agree to meet him, he would escalate his pursuit in some unpredictable way. The walk to the bus stop every evening had become the trailer to a very bad low-budget slasher movie. Everyone she saw was following her, and as it was Kings Cross they all looked pretty weird.

That Monday, she ordered –

Tomorrow
Flisar, Evald
1992
YK.1994.a.13271

– and put it on her book pile.

François Secret replied with –

Four O'Clock, and other stories
MacNeill, Janet
1956
NNN.7820

Whilst looking for the book she eventually chose –

See you tomorrow
Woodford, Peggy
1979
x.990/15647.Woolwich

– she chillingly came across another title –

See you at the Morgue
Blochman, Lawrence Goldtree
1946
NN.63310

The temptation to spy upon whoever walked past her desk whilst she was away from it was great. But the likelihood was that François Secret would see her doing this – and assume she was checking him out.

She went home, didn't eat and didn't sleep much either.

The following morning she couldn't help dressing more smartly than usual. Even if she was meeting a psycho, she wanted to be looking her best. It would give her more authority, she hoped, when she told him to please leave her alone or she would call the police.

And there was always a chance . . .

But no.

She decided to delay her entrance for as long as possible, so left herself most of the day with nothing else to do but stay in her room getting nervous.

It took her a full half an hour to decide that wearing perfume would give out the wrong signals. (But to suggest that she cared about what signals she was giving out might be equally dangerous.)

Around two forty-five, she set off for the bus station. Typically, a Number 73 arrived almost immediately – dropping her off outside the library a quarter of an hour later. She went and hid in the downstairs toilets for the next fifty minutes.

The walk upstairs to the cafeteria (she decided it wasn't safe to take the lift) was the longest she'd endured since the one approaching the notice board in college to find out what her degree was. (A First, her greatest moment.)

She arrived five minutes early. Only a few tables were free, so she decided to get a drink and sit down before they all went in the traditional teatime rush. The worst thing of all would be to endure this confrontation standing up, with everyone around tuning in to what she was saying – with nothing between her and François Secret but air. Her quick glance around the cafeteria hadn't revealed any likely Secrets, but how was she to know.? She bought herself a decaf cappuccino, nervy enough already to make caffeine dangerous, and went to pay. Even if François were sitting there, she wouldn't be able to find him. He would have to either wave her over (oh, horror) or get up from his table and come across to hers.

She walked a little unsteadily to an empty table for two – no chance of any other couple joining them. (Couple? What was she thinking?)

She sat down and closed her eyes, praying she could have a moment's quiet to gather herself. Her fingers pressed into her eyelids. Oh God.

"Hello," said a male voice, almost immediately.

She heard the chair opposite scrape back as he sat down.

Oh God.

François? she almost asked, so much had she come to think of him as that.

His voice hadn't sounded too scary. It had even been, though she couldn't tell why, slightly familiar.

"I'm glad you came," he said.

Although the sudden sound of his voice had made her jump, for some reason she hadn't looked up.

She was sitting there, opposite him, whoever he was, her eyes still pressed by her fingers.

"Aren't you going to even look at me?" he said.

Suddenly, she had an inspiration. Taking her hands away from her face, she said, "No."

"Aren't you curious to see who I am?"

"I can hear who you are perfectly well."

"Then you'll know I'm not a psycho." Now he began to talk very fast, not leaving himself enough time for breath. "It's just that I spotted what you were doing with Heinz the Handsome and I thought it was so funny and clever I thought someone should do it back to you, you see."

"You were a bit more forward than I was," she said.

He replied with the words, "I love you I love you I love you." And for an instant she thought it was a declaration, but he continued by saying, 'Author: Bemelmans, Ludwig.

Published: 1943. Shelfmark: 12332.eee.19. I think that's pretty forward."

She smiled.

"How did you spot me?" she asked.

"I'm a librarian," he said. "We know all our readers' little tricks. You're not the first to use this one, you know."

Now she recognised the voice. And now she could bear to open her eyes and look at him.

He was bald, not too slim, with bad clothes and lovely big brown eyes. The name on his nametag was Mark.

A bunch of bright orange daffodils lay in between them on the tabletop, next to the sugar bowl; a bunch of flowers for her.

"Oh," she said, "hello."

"Hello," Mark said.

She blushed, and looked at the gently subsiding froth on her cappuccino.

End
The End
1863
Mic.A.10075(12)

The River Underground

Richard Tromans

His name was Husman. He came from The Gambia, or Gambia as most people call it. The Gambia is really just a river, the country is just the scrub that stretches out a hundred miles or so on either side of the great river's banks.

Husman had come to England to make money. He'd come just for a few months. He planned to return to his home and build his own compound and be a big player in Baku.

He was here illegally – it was simpler that way. He couldn't afford to get here *and* be turned away. This was to be his once-in-a-lifetime-experience.

He'd been very lucky. He'd made it to London without too many problems. His English was good and he was well prepared. He had talked to many tubabs on the beach in Baku, plus a few from the aid agencies while he was working upcountry teaching English to the kids there.

They'd told him that though he might think that all white people were rich in fact they weren't. Some of the young tourists told him they had no proper job at all.

The tubabs told him people in London got paid more than £100 a week for doing nothing more than looking for work. One told him that he'd taken his £100 a week, plus a little they had in the bank and a bit from doing some work on the side, and had come to Gambia for a one week holiday.

The young tubab said when he returned the free money would still be there. For him it was back to security, back to that city of millions where every tubab seemed to come from.

But where was that free money coming from that these tubabs kept pulling from their pockets? It was like there was a money spring welling up in that cold country. Like a river underground washing up all the money from the world out onto the flood plains of the old River Thames.

The river Gambia never worked like that; it washed people out to other lands and sometimes it brought villagers from upcountry to Baku looking for a new life in the tubab hotels. But not money. No, never money.

Despite the shock of their careless wealth, it did not put him off the tubabs. Most of them, despite their money, never acted impolitely in Gambia. In fact, sometimes, though he could not exactly explain why, they seemed to be nicer to him than they were to each other.

He was fascinated by the prices of things and how much you could earn as a tubab. The best one he ever heard was £3.50 an hour for washing dishes! Were these people insane? Were these people so rampant with their money that they could pay people £3.50 an hour just to run some water over some plates? That was enough money in Gambia to feed the family.

The only tubab Husman didn't like was the aid worker who lived in his compound. He was a tall blonde man and said he was a Christian. He had an African wife, a very pretty one, from Angola.

He'd been in Africa for five years. Been all over the place. He said he loved Africa. Said that he worked for free. "Must be a rich man to work for free," Husman's best friend Captain had said.

Captain was from Liberia. He'd been in the army there and had fled to Gambia. That's why they called him Captain. He'd never talk about what happened in the army so Husman never asked him. But he was a good friend. A real friend.

One day Hus was sitting in the yard mashing up some tea when he heard a conversation in a room nearby.

"One in ten is any good, you know," said the aid worker.

"Yes?" said another English voice, a new one.

"These people, they'll steal anything. You put a gallon of petrol outside in a drum. You come back it's been siphoned half away. You leave your motor scooter out on the street too long and someone unscrews the pedals and walks off with them."

Husman had no answer to the man's complaints, he just didn't understand. Hus was not surprised that the tubab didn't understand.

* * *

After Husman arrived in England he started work as a cleaner in the London Underground. He worked for another company that worked for the Underground and spent all his time cleaning in the tubes.

When he worked the people would pass all around him like he was not there. After the first three or four days he stopped trying to talk to people. They moved too quickly. They had nothing to say to him anyway.

And the people in London – who were these people? People from all over the world. People from every country in Africa, North, South, East, West. And African people who had lived here even before he was born and were as soft and as strange as the regular tubabs.

Captain had said that some of these had come from Gambia long ago, then gone to America as slaves, then the Caribbean as free people and then to London for jobs. It sounded incredible but Captain swore it was true.

Anything seemed possible now he was here in London.

He laughed at the things they used to tell him about tubabs when he was a child. They said that tubabs were so physically weak that you could crush their hands if you held them too hard. And there was some truth in that – their hands were so soft, soft as a little baby's hand, soft as a girl's breasts.

And they had laughed when tubabs talked about men having gone to the moon. Some of the young people in his compound believed it, but the leaders who'd only just come from the family village upcountry, they almost died laughing when you said that to them.

When he got here he saw that it was all true. He read English very well and he read everything he could get his hands on. The newspapers here were so full of things. Especially on a Sunday when they had lots of pictures of beautiful houses, each one as good as the President of Gambia's house.

And most people didn't even appear to work especially hard here to get that kind of thing. He worked hard though.

He'd work either early mornings or late nights. Both were terrible. And now he did believe some of the things the Christian had said about the way things were in England. The Christian had said that England was not all good and happy, that this image was a myth, that it had its own problems with poverty. He had not believed a word of it.

But he had seen children, English children, sleeping in the tubes, taking drugs, selling themselves for sex – worse than anything he had seen in the worst part of Baku.

Craziness was rampant here too. At night there were so many crazy people. It was like the Ju-Ju bird had got into all the people down in the tube. People jumped onto the tube tracks and killed themselves. People were vomiting and fighting and urinating everywhere, every night, like animals in a mad heat – people in suits too with lots of money. And then there were the blind people with just a fat funny dog walking through the tubes on their own and not worrying about a thing. It was a crazy place.

But the money was good. Every week he would take his cheque to the bank and cash it directly. All he needed to show was some ID and they gave him his money. And it was good money.

He lived with three other guys from Gambia in a room in a place called Hackney Downs. He had got there in the summer and that was not too bad. But now, when it was getting cold, it was too harsh.

He was not sure which was worse or being back at the room. In the room all they talked about was home – about the women back at home, about the food back at home, and about the sound of the sea and the fishing boats and the taste of real milk and real sugar and real couscous.

Milk at home was so thick, and the cream floated in it and melted on your tongue. Here the milk was like water and the sugar like dust.

TV was also mixed. The animal programmes were the funniest. There was a cat – it had a broken leg – the family and two doctors spent a month looking after it. X-rays and drugs and all the full treatment.

Hus remembered when his cousin broke his leg and it wasn't done right at the clinic and he found it hard to marry because his leg was never right. And then he thought about this little cat.

And the tubabs begged here too – even the ones who already had the free money. They asked him for money when he was coming home from work. He had been taught that Allah wanted him to be gracious to the poor, but this was too much.

Sometimes on Friday nights they would go and buy some ganja. Not very good stuff, not like they grew back at home, but they would smoke it and sing together a bit and talk about who was the better Wailer.

Although some of his brothers liked the Nigerian-style guitar music, he and his friends loved the old reggae best and no one could change their minds.

The hardest thing was finding somewhere to keep the money they had saved. Hus would save his up until he had three or four weeks' money then get it wired to the bank in Gambia. It was an excellent system. He wired it to his own name. He'd pick it up from there when he got home. They charged him a lot – but it was safe.

One man, from Senegal, in another room on the floor above, went crazy one Saturday morning. His savings had been taken. He'd put them under a floorboard. He threatened everyone near him with a knife. He had been planning to go home in two or three weeks. Now he would have to stay.

The police came and it was a bad scene for everyone. After they arrested the man from Senegal they wanted to know who everyone else was. They wanted to see papers. Hus was lucky that morning. He was just coming back from the night-shift and when he saw the police outside the flats he just kept walking and sat in a McDonalds for an hour with a cup of tea and read the morning papers.

It was like that sometimes – feeling like he was doing a slow bank robbery, and at any time, as if responding to a call from months ago, the police were going to arrive and take him away.

It was not so bad now, though. He'd been able to send back enough money to pay for the blocks and cement for a half compound with two rows of rooms.

He couldn't wait to see Captain's face when he got back. Captain would be given the second biggest room. The biggest, of course, would be for him and his wife – whoever she would be.

The threat of return was not too unbearable. He had to get back sometime someday anyway.

Unlike some of the people he met in London he had no intention of staying. He could have made this place home if he had wanted to, but he'd rather be a rich man at home than a poor man here for the rest of his life.

In Baku he was a teacher, respected, well-paid. No, when the time was right he would go back to his friends. The police might even give him a free flight home if he was arrested for working illegally. He'd heard of such things. It was quite kind of them really. He couldn't imagine the Gambian police giving a tubab a free flight.

Though the work was dull the money was coming in steadily and nicely. The cleaning manager was friendly and he never stole their money and never cheated. He just had to endure this for another three months, he reckoned.

* * *

For another month life carried on as usual. But then, just two months from the trip home, he came across something that he had never expected. He fell in love. With a tubab.

He was cleaning the platform one night at Farringdon. He was getting to the end of the platform when he noticed a lady sitting on one of the benches. She was crying. Her big black coat was drawn up around her cheeks and her blonde bob of hair hanging down over her face.

She dropped a tissue as he approached. Hus put out his metal gripper-stick and went to grab it.

"Sorry," she said.

"That's OK," said Hus and snatched it up and swished it into his bag.

"Sorry about that," she said.

"It's no problem. If you didn't drop things I'd have nothing to pick up," said Hus and stood up straight to look at her properly.

She looked up at him. Her nose and eyes were red and wet. Her face was pale though, even for a tubab.

He wasn't that tall, about 5'8", but he was well-built and kept an air of dexterity and dignity about him despite the overalls and the bag of rubbish.

"Excuse me, but are you alright?" asked Hus.

She made no reply. Instead she delved into her pocket and yanked out another tissue and placed it over her nose.

Hus took this as the typical sociability of Londoners and carried on his way to the end of the platform. As he got to the end a train came in, loud and heavy, then rolled out again.

He was surprised to see that the lady was still there. He headed back towards her on his way to the stairs.

"Excuse me?" said the lady as he walked past her.

"Yes?"

"You like your job?"

"Excuse me?"

"You like your job?"

"It's OK," said Hus.

She smiled a strange smile and made no further questions.

"What am I doing?," she thought. "Talking to a cleaner – an immigrant cleaner too, judging by his accent. What the hell am I trying to do having a conversation with someone like him? It's like those people who stop once a month to have a long chat with a *Big Issue* seller, as if they were making a point about how good they were. I hate that kind of thing."

But right now she needed to talk to someone. Maybe those kind of people did too.

"Excuse me?" she said.

Hus was getting a little nervous about this woman now.

"Yes," he said and turned back to face her.

"You like your job?"

"You've already asked me that question. I don't mean to be rude – but what do you want?"

"Sorry, I'm sorry."

"No need to be sorry. Look, I have to go and clean that other platform, excuse me."

"It was nice talking to you," she said softly as he walked away.

Hus walked to the start of the platform and up the steps by the barriers and then down again onto the platform going the other way.

The new platform wasn't too bad. Now winter was coming there was less litter and Farringdon was never that bad anyway – it was mostly business people and they were quite good about dropping things. Their only bad habit was dropping the morning paper.

Halfway along the other platform he looked up from his duties. There she was, still sitting on the bench. At least one more train had gone past since he'd started on this side. When she saw he'd noticed her she gave him another funny smile. Then she gave a little wave like Hus would give to a child.

He acknowledged her with a smile but carried on. When he was level with her the woman stood up as if to watch him better, like she was at a football match.

"It looks good," she shouted over the tube rails between them.

"What?"

"The platform looks pretty good now."

"Excuse me, lady, but are you having a joke with me?"

Hus didn't like this sudden attention from the tubab – it made no sense what she was doing. It had nothing to do with him getting his money and getting back to Gambia. It had nothing to do with his life. She was part of the tubab world; he was not a member of it, he was just passing through, like a tube train and he liked that.

"What's your name?" she shouted over the rails.

Really, this was too much.

A would-be passenger on a bench on Hus' platform looked up from his drunken Friday night stupor and stared across at her.

"No, not you," she said.

"My name is Husman."

"My name's Paul," added the drunk in the blue suit.

"I think she is talking to me," said Hus.

"Fuck off," said Paul and stared at him with violent intent.

"Don't talk to me like that."

"Fuck off. Here, pick that up,' said Paul and threw an empty cigarette packet he'd found in his pocket onto the floor.

It was not worth a confrontation. Hus carried on to the end of the platform, but more quickly now.

The girl kept quiet and the drunk immediately sank back into a stupor.

Hus hurried to finish off the platform. He wanted to get out of here.

More trains came and went in both directions.

He had soon finished.

He headed past the drunk, who had his eyes firmly closed now, and back up to the barriers. The last job was the ticket room floor. But before he could get started on it the girl had appeared.

She was about the same height as him and her heels were lifting her slightly forwards. She was smiling and her eyes were dry now.

Hus decided he wouldn't stand for any more silliness. He walked straight up to her. She just kept on staring at him.

"Excuse me, lady, but what do you want?" said Hus and rested his gripper on the floor.

"Want to go for a drink?" she said chirpily.

"A drink?" Hus said incredulously.

"A drink. A beer. With me?"

"I don't drink alcohol."

"Have a Coke then. When do you get off work?"

"In about half an hour," Hus told her but couldn't believe he was saying it.

"Well, I'll wait for you."

Hus grappled in shock for something to say.

"But I don't know you. What's your name?" he finally managed.

"Helen, my name's Helen."

Hus picked up the discarded tickets and crisp packets and fag ends and gum and old papers and Helen waited by the ticket machine for him. When he finished he stowed his stuff, got out of his overall and went over to meet her.

Hus felt a faint warmth running through his limbs. He felt that he was walking close to a very deep ravine and the view was beautiful and frightening at the same time.

They walked into a nearby wine bar, one he'd passed many times but never considered going into. It wasn't very crowded, it was more of an after-work place, and it was getting late. Hus went and sat on a free sofa in the corner while Helen got some drinks from the long marble bar.

She placed the drinks on a small glass table between them and dropped her coat off across the back of her chair. When she settled he saw that her lips were holding back a hundred questions.

Hus beat her to it.

"So, what do you want?" he said as coldly as he could.

She had to be up to something. It was just not possible this had anything genuine about it. Tubabs did not do things like this without a reason. Maybe it was some kind of trick? Maybe she was with the police?

"How about I just ask you a question and then you ask me one?" she said.

She beamed him a long smile along with her question. She wasn't going to be put off by his fake chill.

Hus picked his Coke up and sipped it slowly. As he drank he looked nervously around the room. Everyone was white, well-dressed and no one was paying them any attention. He watched people buying drinks from the long bar with its tall vase stuffed with expensive flowers. Everyone seemed in their place – a man buying cigarettes from a machine, an old man with a young woman who kept giggling at everything he said, a group of loud men around a table laughing together. It looked safe.

"OK. I go first," said Hus.

She nodded and leant back in her seat a bit.

"Why were you crying?"

"You cheat. You can't ask me that as my first question. Ask me another."

Hus grinned.

"Why were you crying?"

She sighed but decided to answer.

"Because I was lonely."

Before Hus could ask any more she had spoken.

"What is a smart guy like you picking up rubbish for?"

"How do you know I'm smart?"

"You sound it."

"Are you the police?"

She frowned. She was smart too.

"So, you're an illegal immigrant. That explains something. Without going into too many details – I'm right, aren't I?"

Hus nodded admiringly.

"My question again. Why were you crying?"

"Would you believe me if I told you I was thinking of throwing myself in front of a train? And by the way, this is the first, well almost the first time, I have ever done anything like this – inviting a total stranger for a drink, that is. It's definitely the first time I've ever thought about throwing myself under a tube train."

They ended up having a few drinks: Hus drank more Coke and she drank more gin and tonic. Helen was getting a bit drunk when Hus called time.

"I have to go now, I have an early shift tomorrow."

"When do you get off?"

"At four. I'm at Liverpool Street station tomorrow."

"Can I come and meet you by the ticket machines again?"

"Well, that's kind of you, but I usually go straight to bed for a few hours after I finish the early shift. Maybe I could see you after that?"

"Maybe I could meet you at four and then come straight along to bed with you?"

She immediately saw she'd made a mistake. Hus told himself he should have known this would be the result of the drink.

Then, without any connection to the big frown on his face Hus's mouth started to turn into a grin. He felt a rush of excitement and the frown smoothed away and let his grin takeover.

"Why not?" he thought.

But he didn't like the idea of her coming back to his room, not with Moma and his friends there. They'd like it though. He toyed with the idea for a few moments. Him walking in with Helen on his arm. "Excuse me, boys," he would say, "I need some privacy."

It wouldn't work. Moma would probably start off in Mandinka and make some bad jokes and embarrass him. Besides, the room was dirty and the flats were in a bad area. She wouldn't want to go there.

"I'll meet you in the evening and then we can go to your place," said Hus. "What about that?"

"Meet you Liverpool Street tube, eight p.m.?"

"If you don't come I can do a bit of overtime."

He didn't tell Moma. After he finished his early shift he slept, got cleaned up and put on his best – a jacket he'd got from a charity shop that really suited him and some old leather slip-on shoes he'd borrowed from Sebo. He got back to Liverpool Street half an hour early. The ticket staff didn't even recognize him.

She was late but she looked beautiful. Hus couldn't see what she had done but she looked so much sharper than the night before. She wanted to go to a restaurant. Hus had anticipated this. He had no spare money – especially none to spend on restaurants.

"I'm not sure if I feel hungry," said Hus.

Helen had anticipated this as well.

"Look, I buy this one and you get the next one, OK?"

She didn't expect him to want to see her again.

Hus agreed and they went to an Indian restaurant on Brick Lane. Hus didn't like his meal at all and they finished it quickly.

She paid and they went and stood on the pavement outside, neither speaking, both waiting. Then came the moment. Both felt the whole thing was so obvious neither wanted to say it. Eventually Helen led the way.

"Come on, let's go back to my house."

Hus said nothing and just followed her to a taxi rank.

She paid for the taxi and then they went up to her flat. It was a large flat in a big old house in Islington. It was nice inside. Made out to look like the pictures in the Sunday magazines. It was all in bright colours and had a smooth varnished wooden floor and tiny lights all over the ceiling.

She'd not told him what she did, just that she had a good job in the City and that she was single and had nothing much to spend her money on so she bought stuff for her home.

"It's funny, I just got dressed here an hour ago," said Helen as she sat on her favourite chair, a huge green leather armchair.

Hus sat opposite her on a wooden chair by a table.

They sat like that for a few seconds, just looking at each other.

She had run out of things to ask him. He'd told her all about Gambia, as much as he wanted to tell any way, and how he got here and how he'd get back and what he was going to do with the money and about his friends and his family. She had dodged his questions though, every time.

Hus did not mind her just wanting to sleep with him. A lot of tubab women came to Gambia just to have sex with the men there. Especially old Scandinavian women, they were rampant there. What he minded was her not sharing anything with him. He didn't like the feeling.

Hus finally knew he had to speak and felt the blood rush to his cheeks.

"Helen, you're a very nice person, but I want to say that if you don't tell me what you're doing I'm going to leave right now."

"What do you mean?" she said and leant forwards, blushing too.

"Why did you invite me here?"

"Come on, Husman, don't be naïve."

"No, not that. We both know that side of things. I want to know why you want us to do what we're doing."

"You want the story? The whole story?"

"Yes. You're the first tubab woman I have known like this and I don't understand you. I want to understand you."

Then he added something she hadn't expected.

"I want to understand you before anything happens."

"OK," she said, even blushing more than before.

"I was going to throw myself in front of the train because my husband has left me and I've lost my job and I don't know anyone any more in this bloody horrible city. Not that I really would have done it. I'm not really like that. I just feel so horribly lonely."

Hus looked at her and then around the room for signs of a husband – there were none. He wasn't sure if he believed her.

"If you're looking for his stuff I threw it all away, that which he didn't take with him."

"When did he go?"

"Three months ago and you're the first person to visit me in my house since he left."

"And the job?"

"I couldn't do it any more. We worked in the same company. Everyone there says it's my fault."

She coughed, put a hand to her face, then regained her control.

"And it was. I slept with one of his friends. Now none of them will talk to me. I'm totally lonely. I haven't even told my parents or friends back home yet. I kept thinking that it was going to be OK again. But – well, you can see. It's just me now."

"Why'd you sleep with one of his friends?"

Hus felt like taking it as far as he could – he wanted to at last get inside the head of one of these tubabs.

"He was nice. We were at a party, me and Graham, my husband. Things haven't been going . . . *weren't* going well, between us for a long time. It just happened, there at the party.

"Then Graham found out and that was it. I never thought he was that kind of man. But it hurt him. And he left. I couldn't face seeing him at work. We work on different floors, but it was too much."

"And the friend?"

"Graham has never talked to him since."

"And me, what about me?"

"I don't know yet. At least we haven't done anything to make either of us feel guilty."

"Then I think we should," Hus said.

Hus stood up and walked over the Persian rug that lay between them.

* * *

He stayed with her that night, and the next. The third night he spent at his house. Moma gave him a hard time when he came in. He only just managed to convince his roommate he was only doing extra-long hours.

The fourth night he was back at hers. After that she said she didn't want him to spend any more nights away from her. So he stayed there every night.

He carried on working and during the day she kept herself busy by hunting for a new job. He'd work hard each shift then get the bus to her house. When he came through the door they'd go straight to the bedroom, strip and make love until they fell asleep.

After two weeks she suggested that Hus move in with her. Her certainty wasn't going to invite her to move in with him and Moma. He agreed and arrived with his suitcase.

After three weeks she started a new job and tried to persuade him to give up his job so he could relax at home. Money was not a problem, she said. But he wouldn't do it. It was embarrassing enough as it was that he was living in *her* house and that it was *she* who paid for everything.

After five weeks, they had settled down into a regular rhythm of life and Hus was getting used to living in a fancy central London flat with a beautiful woman who earned £60,000.

She came home very late some nights and was often exhausted from her days at work, but she was always pleased to see him and he was always pleased to see her.

He did not think about how the relationship would end, or the imbalance created by her wealth, he just let it happen. It was so easy to let it happen. It would not stop him from going back though, he told himself.

Then one day it all stopped. One afternoon when he was home on his own the doorbell rang. He'd just finished his morning shift and had been in the shower. The central heating was on full power and he was wandering about the house with a white towel wrapped around his hips and a toothbrush wedged in the corner of his mouth. The stereo was cranked up loud and Hus was feeling the best he'd felt since arriving in this strange city.

The doorbell rang again. He heard it the second time. Hus turned the music down and went over to the intercom.

"Helen?" said a man's nervous voice.

"She's not in yet," said Hus, his words garbled by the toothbrush in his mouth.

"Sorry, wrong number," said the man and the intercom clicked off.

Hus was just walking back to the bathroom when the buzzer went again.

"Helen?" said the man, this time more loudly.

Hus took the toothbrush out.

"She's not in yet."

"Who's that?"

The stranger's voice had suddenly become nasty.

"I'm a friend of Helen's, what's the message?" said Hus and waited for a response.

There was no message. The caller let go of the talk button.

Hus went back into the bedroom and picked up another towel to do his back. He knew who it was, he could feel the man's jealousy through the walls of the flat. He had been waiting for this day. Now he didn't know what he was going to do. There was nothing he could do.

Hus rubbed his back.

Maybe the man would not come back. Maybe that was it.

He went back into the bathroom to put the toothbrush away.

When he walked back into the lounge there was a dark-haired tubab in a pinstriped suit standing there. He was holding a leather briefcase in one hand, a bunch of house keys in the other.

"So I suppose you're Graham," said Hus and tucked a thumb into the towel around his waist.

"Yes I am. And who the fuck are you?" said Graham and dropped his briefcase on the floor with a clatter.

"I live here. I'm Husman."

The man's face was going very red. He seemed bewildered. Sweat sprang from deep within his head and popped out over his skin. He looked this way and that for an answer. Finally he managed to look Husman in the face.

"You're living with Helen?"

Hus nodded.

The man looked at the floor. He began to breathe very deeply. When he looked up he was close to tears.

"Get out of my flat!" he hissed.

"Sorry, but this is not your flat any more."

That statement seemed to help suddenly. Graham grew calm and a thin smile lined his face as if a wonderful idea had come to him.

"Actually, this flat *is* mine."

"It's Helen's," said Hus uncertainly, sensing a problem.

"No, it's mine. Very much mine, I'm afraid. So, I think you're going to have to leave. Let's say, er, in about two minutes."

"You left her, man, you can't come back now," said Hus.

"What do you mean, I can't come back now? What did she tell you? I was dead? And what are you going to do about it anyway? Fight me for her? Don't be stupid. Look, you've got to go."

Hus bit on his bottom lip and sized up the husband.

"She doesn't want you any more. OK? If she wanted you why is she with me?"

This made Graham crazy again.

"Get out of my house!"

"No, you get out of her house."

Graham put out an arm, stepped towards him and shoved Hus backwards.

"You want to fight?" asked Hus.

Graham just pushed him again.

Hus swung a left fist into Graham's face, then before his opponent could move he followed it with a right. Graham lamely swung out and missed. Hus put a left into his stomach and that was it. The tubab doubled over and Hus brought down a sharp right, this time to the temple, flooring him at his feet.

As Hus stood over him Graham quietly got up. Totally ignoring the victor's presence he picked up his things and left the flat.

"What did he say?" said Helen as soon as Hus told her about the visit.

"Nothing, except this was his flat and he wanted me out in two minutes."

"What happened?"

"I got rid of him."

"How?"

He told her. She was not happy. Then she did a bit of explaining. Technically this *was* his flat – he had bought it some years ago. Also, they had not divorced, just separated. Graham was totally in the right, she said. Why had Hus had to hit him? Her husband was not a violent man, she said. She'd have to call him and sort things out, she said. She also warned Hus that her husband was not likely to give up.

Hus said nothing.

For the rest of the week she acted strangely. He tried to make love to her but she pushed him away. She sulked. Then a week later she was happy again.

One night she turned to him. "Hus, I've been thinking. I think I need to have some space again. I need to think about what I'm doing."

"You want me to move out?"

"Well, just for a few weeks."

"So you can go back to him?"

Hus was furious.

"No - so I can think. I need to think about what I'm doing."

"So you can go back with him – that's what it is."

"No, it's not that."

"Yes, it is."

Hus moved close to her and looked into her blue-grey eyes.

"I don't trust you, Helen."

"Then go then!" she shouted and stomped into the bathroom.

Later that night he was sitting with Moma getting very high back in the room in Hackney. He didn't want to talk about it, but Moma kept asking, so he told him. He tried to laugh about it – like it had been all gains for him. But he knew he wanted her and that this foolish relationship had messed him up good.

The next day he didn't go to work. It was not a problem. It was the first day he'd ever taken off and nobody minded. The next day he went back to work as usual and got down to cleaning. But there was something biting at him. He didn't want to pick up these tubabs' rubbish anymore.

"Why should I pick up these people's litter?" he kept asking himself. "Who do they think they are?"

When someone dropped a piece of litter near him he would stand up tall and straight and stare at them hard and long until they knew he was angry at them.

Two nights later he called Helen.

"Helen, what are you doing to me?"

"Me doing to you? What are you doing to *me*?"

"It was you who told me to leave."

"And what about you? I never asked you to move in with me. I never asked to pay for everything. I never asked you to attack my husband."

He could not believe what he was hearing. He tried to argue, she didn't listen. Then he heard it. His voice. The husband's voice.

"My husband wants to talk to you."

There was a horrible pause and then the sound of man's breathing as he handled the phone.

"Right, now look, Husman, my wife doesn't want to see you any more. OK? She doesn't want to see you. If you come near her again we'll call the police. She's told me all about you. I know where you work, where you live, how you don't have a visa. So let us reach an understanding. You stay away from us and no one will know about you, OK?"

"You can't threaten me," said Hus.

"Yes I can, and I just have. I don't give a damn what you do. Stay here all your life if you like. But come near Helen again and you've had it."

Work the next day was almost impossible. Each piece of litter was an insult, every left-behind newspaper a challenge to him. He couldn't do this any more. He had to go home.

There was enough money in that bank in Gambia to do what he'd planned. Except – except now, he didn't want a compound in Baku anymore.

He decided he would try one more time. He went to the flat.

"Hello?" said Helen's voice on the intercom.

"It's Hus. Just let me in. I need to say something to you."

"Hus, I'm sorry. But I think we have to forget about us."

"Helen, you can't treat me like this."

"But Hus, I'm married. You knew it wasn't going to last."

"Let me in."

"No, Hus. I have to move on now. I have to, and you do too."

"I'm not leaving until you see me."

"No, Hus. Please don't do this. If you care about me you'll just go."

Hus took his finger off the buzzer and walked across the road and sat on a low wall opposite the flats. He sat there for an hour, then another. He stared at each white person who walked past him. He stayed there until he was so cold he was shivering. Then he went home.

The next day, just an hour into his shift, there was a deep voice behind him.

"Husman Bari?"

"Yes," said Hus and turned around to see two heavily-built policemen with a middle-aged woman in a beige jacket clutching a piece of paper.

"We are arresting you on suspicion of being an illegal immigrant to this country," one of the policemen said.

"What?" said Hus and dropped his bag and gripper.

Then the other policeman started to read him his rights.

He felt his heart tighten in his chest. He looked into the face of the woman and appealed to her.

Her powdered face gave no sympathy, if anything it grew sterner.

"Mr Bari, do you understand English?" she said.

"Yes."

"Will you come with us voluntarily?"

He nodded.

They walked him up the stairs and out into the cold liquid daylight. Hus felt like he was floating, floating up from a river underground.

The Artist

Maggie Gee

When Isaac had only been with her a month, he came in from the garden holding a rose, a dark red complicated knot of velvet. Bowing slightly, he placed it in her fingers. "Broke in accident," he explained – of course, he was re-pointing the brick at the back – but he handed her own rose over to her with a graceful, cavalier flourish.

"Beautiful, Isaac," she said, inhaling deeply, once, then again. The scent was so intense it shocked her, made her throat catch and her eyes prickle, as if life was suddenly all around her, as if she was breathing for the first time in years. Mary had hay fever, and avoided flowers. "So beautiful – " she did not know what to say. "So beautiful, I shall write about it." (She wrote novels, which had never been published, but she had a study, and told people she wrote.)

"I am artist," said Isaac, grinning at her with self-deprecating, dark-eyed charm. His teeth were very white, but one was chipped; he had a handsome, cherubic face. He lit up before she had noticed; she was always just too late. "I am artist, you see, Mary. I am artist like you." He jabbed his brown finger towards her, laughing. "I make beautiful house for you."

"Wonderful, Isaac. Thank you. But really I just need the tiles laying out in squares."

"Mary, I like you very much. I make you a beautiful floor, it is my present to you.'

"No, really, Isaac. Just squares. One black, one white, one black, one white. As we agreed."

"Don't worry Mary, you will be very happy. See what I will do." He touched his head, indicating wisdom. She smiled at him; he was such a child. He crushed his cigarette into his saucer.

"Really, I'd prefer you to smoke in the garden, Isaac."

"Mary, I do everything – what – you want." He bowed extravagantly, a knight. How old was he? Forty, fifty? "I do it." Then, thinking of something else, eyes veering away, he took out another cigarette, tapping it thoughtfully on the packet.

"I make you a build, for your garden. Where you write your story. I put everything what you want. Very beautiful. I paint it. Put roof, everything."

"Isaac, really, I'm quite happy with my study. We're not allowed to build in the garden."

He nodded, impatient, lit his cigarette, then smiled at her rapturously, transformed. "I have friend, he will be here tomorrow. Or next week, is certain thing. Why I not think of him before? From home, you understand. Very cheap, like me. He will put bookshelves in this build, in your garden. Is a genius. You love him, Mary."

She began to feel tired, though she was laughing. "No. *Really*. About the floor, Isaac – " Hearing the word "floor", he smiled and smoothed out the piece of squared paper where he had sketched out an elaborately crenellated cruciform arrangement of black squares on white, and held it in front of her nose. The smoke irritated her chest.

"You see, now you agree" he said to her. "I am artist. You don't want one square – two square, one square – two square, everything, always. Very boring. No good!"

She took the paper from him, folded it narrowly, and slipped it back into the pocket of his jacket. His eyes looked at her hand on his jacket, then up to her face, and then back to her hand, calculating, flirtatious, but she ignored him. "That's just what I want. Black, white, black, white. Like a chessboard. Very simple. The tiles are in the garage. Now, I must go and work. Please open a window."

Isaac drew a deep, indignant puff on his cigarette, then smiled at her forgivingly. "Yes, you do your work, Mary, you write your books, beautiful. I like this very much, to work for an artist, like me. You are not practical, but never matter. I am practical AND artist."

The rose was lovely, though slightly battered. She kissed it lightly before throwing it away.

"He's impossible,' she complained lazily to her husband as she lay in bed with her book, enjoying the soft snow of the pillow behind shoulders tired from typing, looking at Edward over her glasses, his familiar pinched profile in the cool blue room. She wanted to tell him, she wanted to tell someone, that Isaac had given her a rose, but she couldn't think how to do it. (Why did Edward always lie *on top* of the bedclothes to read? Her feet were cold, his feet were hot. If he came into the bed he could warm her feet up, but Edward was sometimes difficult. For example, the question of holidays. He would never take her on holiday. When they were first married, money was tight, but they hadn't had to worry since his Ma died. A nice little windfall, three hundred thou. And Edward earned extra with consultancy work. But he was – well, careful. In fact, he was mean. So her desire to travel had gradually withered.) "Impossible. Edward? I'm talking to you."

"Who is? For heaven's sake, I'm reading my book."

"Isaac," she said.

He sat up and stared at her. "Why do you keep talking about this *person*? If he's no good, get rid of him. You let these people run you around. Get a proper builder, an English one."

"I tried, if you remember."

"What do you mean?"

"You said the price was outrageous. Isaac is cheap. When you heard his quote, you were very happy."

"You found him, not me."

"I didn't; he put a piece of paper through the door. You agreed we should ask him."

Edward couldn't deny it. He changed tack. "You can't manage tradesmen, you never could. The cleaners never do what you tell them to."

"I haven't got a cleaner. They always leave. Because you won't let me pay them enough."

"You're absolutely hopeless at getting what you want. Just let me talk to him. I'll sort him out."

"– No, Edward. It's fine, really." She knew how Edward would talk to Isaac. He would send him away, as he had threatened to do. Then the house would be empty every day, and the small tasks would remain undone, since Edward thought they were beneath him. Isaac brought something to the house: different smells, not just roses, but tobacco and sweat and maleness and smoke, paint and white spirit and garlic and sausage. She liked his voice, and his accent, which spoke to her of strange wide spaces somewhere far away in southeast Europe, hot stony fields, bright market-places, somewhere she would never go, she supposed, since now she so rarely went out at all. It had slowly crept up on her, or crept around her; her life had shrunk. There was only the house.

"Why do you put up with these fellows, Mary?"

"Well, he does try. And Isaac's – different." (Of course she could never have mentioned the rose. Her memory of it wilted, faded.)

"What the hell does that mean?" How scornfully he spoke. Had he always spoken to her like that?

"Isaac feels he's an artist. He isn't, of course. But he wants to be." She enjoyed this thought. Poor Isaac. What Mary did, he dreamed of.

"Fraud and con-man, like all the others. I want him out by the end of the week. Now could I *please* get on with my book?"

But she saw he was reading his *Antiques Almanac*, which surely could not have much of a plot-line. "He lost everything, you know. In that bloody awful war. He didn't choose to come here. But now we can help him." Saying it, Mary was suffused with love.

Edward sighed with irritation. "He's just an illegal."

She looked at him with hatred; he stripped everything away. Their eyes met, sharp, and darted back into the shadows.

"That's why you're using him. Because he's cheap." He snapped his book shut, lay down abruptly, and presented her with his navy silk back, taking off his glasses, clicking down the arms. "A guy in the office said Afghans are cheaper. Good night, Mary." In minutes he was snoring, the deep round trombones of a man who slept soundly.

But she was left restless, remembering the rose. Isaac was a child, but she had to have someone.

In September, when he should have been clearing out the drains, Isaac had brought round his wife and daughter in a rusty, dust-covered grey saloon. He didn't come at eight, his usual time, but the doorbell rang at ten, and he was there on the step.

"Van break down. Very sorry."

"Never mind, come in and get started."

"No can do. I am in car, with wife, daughter . . . I can come in for cup of coffee, Mary, only."

Isaac loved her real coffee, which reminded him of home. "Actually I'm writing," she protested, but he had already barrelled past her, sighing.

"What about your wife, your daughter?"

"They are well, thank you, Mary. Except only daughter – "

" I mean, you can't leave them out in the car, Isaac." It was a bore, but good manners demanded it.

"Yes, they love it."

"Of course they don't love it. Go and ask them in."

"No, please, Mary . . . "

"I insist."

They trooped up the path, very straight-faced, in front of Isaac, who drove them before him like sheep, looking off contemptuously to one side with a smile that seemed to say to the neighbours, "I know, but these were all I could get." "Wife," he jabbed one finger towards a thickset, grey-faced woman with hostile, uncomprehending eyes. "Daughter," and he put his hand on the girl's shoulder, but this time his voice was tinged with love and regret. "Anna," he added. "Seventeen." She was pretty, with her father's white teeth and cherub nose, but her skin and lips were pale, too pale, her eyes had a slightly sunken look, her hair was flat and yellow, and she leaned on her mother, as if she had no bones to stand up.

"Hallo, Anna," Mary smiled at the daughter, who almost smiled back, but then bit her lip and looked down. To the wife she tried "I'm sorry, I don't know your name", but the words the woman gave were guttural, unfamiliar, and Mary could turn it into nothing she could use or remember.

"Will they have tea or coffee?" she asked Isaac.

"No, they don't like," said Isaac, pushing them into the drawing-room, while trying to shepherd Mary back into the dining-room where the serious business of coffee would go on.

"Lemonade? Biscuits?"

"They don't want."

"Water? Honestly, Isaac, they must do."

Mary had broken away from Isaac, doing her duty, reluctantly, and followed the two women into the drawing-room, where she found them standing together in front of the fireplace. The mother appeared to be confiding something urgent: the daughter was placating her, and staring round the room. "Sit down," Mary said, and they did, too promptly. "Cake? Fruit juice? Milk? Herbal tea?"

The daughter took pity on her and explained. "My mother speaks nothing," she said. "I like water, thank you, only water." Mary noticed a flimsy golden cross round her neck with a fleck of diamante like a tear at the centre. "Water, lovely," Mary said, gratefully. "And your mother, would she like coffee like your father?"

"No, she likes the toilet," said the daughter.

"Er, it's upstairs," said Mary. "That is to say, we are extending the downstairs one." They looked at her blankly. She gave up. "Upstairs. I'll show you."

There was confabulation between the two women in their own language. "No, she goes quick alone," said the daughter hastily.

Mary brought water for Anna and went back to brew coffee for Isaac, who was inspecting, with what was surely self-conscious over-emphasis, the prints on the walls of the dining-room, frowning up, pursing his lips, nodding judiciously. "Yes, very beautiful," he said aloud, looking, not by accident, she thought, at a Lucian Freud of a naked woman. He must want her to see that he liked bare flesh. Such a terrible flirt! Though of course, she was flattered . . . Isaac wouldn't grasp Freud's darker themes. He made as if to notice her a few seconds later. "Daughter is ill," he hissed.

"Oh dear, Isaac."

"Yes, I take to the doctor. They can do nothing."

Did he mean she was dying? A moment's inspection of his vigorously furrowed brow told her it couldn't be as serious as that. "She need clean air. Air here very dirty. She cannot breathe, Mary. London very bad. Is dust, where we live, damp also. No good."

"Oh, has she got asthma? What a shame – "

"Asthma, yes. In my country, she hasn't got it. Now she pray every day to Virgin, but she get it very bad." He imitated the sound of an aged saw.

She brought their coffee. The wife was still upstairs. Mary tried not to think anxious thoughts about her jewellery. Isaac slumped at the table, his strong thighs splayed.

"I am so sorry, Isaac. But don't worry. I myself have atrocious hay fever. They're all allergies. The doctors can help you. Have you considered acupuncture?" She mimed little needles jabbing into her arm.

He shook his heavy, curly head mournfully. “Injection? No. More coffee, please.”

“Is your wife all right?”

“Yes, is only daughter who is ill.”

“No, I mean *is she all right upstairs?*”

“Oh yes, she just eat too many apples, and it all comes ph-th-ph-th-ph-th-ph-th-uh out again, Mary.”

“Ah.” Mary’s social skills were defeated. The apples, unfortunately, came from their garden. They’d forgotten to pick them, so Isaac had done so, taking away half of them, much more than was agreed. Isaac did have a rapacious side. She changed the subject back to Anna. “Your daughter looks very pale and tired.”

“Yes, of course. Always tired, Anna.”

“Really? I didn’t know asthma did that.”

“No, is not asthma, honestly. Anna is young, seventeen.”

“But young people shouldn’t be tired, Isaac.”

“No, Mary. Problem is . . . Daughter has already daughter.”

“*Is* already daughter?”

“Daughter has baby.”

“*Is* a baby,” Mary said. It was extraordinary how they muddled “is” and “has”, such a simple mistake, but he often seemed to make it. “She’s hardly a baby, at seventeen.”

He was still looking at her, mystified. “I love the baby,” he insisted.

There was an obtuseness about these people. “She has to grow up some time,” Mary said.

Invited in, at first, on a strictly limited basis, to re-point the brick, then re-paint the drawing room, Isaac’s role slowly became a roving one, as different parts of the house demanded his attention. He would announce these impending tasks to Mary, with a mixture of sorrow and glee. Of course he could sort it out. Of course for him it was no problem. But on various occasions he needed “my very good friend", this or that "genius" at fixing wood or wiring, always a different one, always from back home.

Their relationship progressed in fits and starts. Isaac nearly always complimented her. She had striking blue eyes, she had always known that, but he noticed the effect of different colours that she wore, and one day told her he would like to paint her. "First paint my house," she said, fondly, and he looked at her with a strange regret that made her think he was a little in love. It wasn't so surprising; she was still quite pretty, and his benefactor, and a writer. But her books became a stumbling block. Isaac took everything literally; she had told him she wrote books, when he first came to the house. After a few months, he asked if he could see one, to flatter her, of course, and she deflected it. But he kept on asking, becoming more pressing, and in the end she had been forced to explain: she had not actually published any books. He seemed unreasonably disappointed. Was there a slight dimming of his admiration?

Isaac had been with them for thirteen months when Edward put his foot down. Isaac was doing the exterior paint at the back; a wet July had meant a sequence of days when he arrived hopeful at eight in the morning but put down his brushes at ten or eleven with the first small splashes of summer rain. Edward's birthday was coming at the end of the month. He expected a big lunch party in the garden.

"When will this clown get the job finished?" he raged at his wife.

"It's been very wet."

"It isn't now. Has he been here today?"

"His daughter's been ill this week, so he's hardly been in," Mary said, placatingly, but Edward glared at Isaac's paint-pots straggling across the patio, and his brushes in tins of untidy white spirit, sticking up at the sky at an irritating angle.

"If he doesn't get the bloody job done and this mess out of the way before Friday, he's never going to cross my threshold again!" he exploded. "I mean it, Mary. Don't think I don't. We'll get in a decent English builder. At last."

Next day Isaac arrived around four, looking worried. After giving up for months, he smelled of smoke again. "Anna is in the hospital," he explained. "I just come to tell you how she is, Mary."

She didn't make him tea. "Edward says you have to finish the painting by Friday or never come back, and he means it," she said.

"She is very bad, Mary. Tea with sugar, please."

"No, he is *serious,*" she said. "You have to get it done."

He was going to light up. She took the cigarette from his hand, but he suddenly clutched her fingers, with an odd little moan. "Last night they make us stay with her in hospital. Baby is with friend crying, crying, crying. Daughter look like daughter's daughter. Face goes blue . . . "

She pulled her hand away. "Isaac, what are you going to do?" she yelled at him, feeling her power at last, losing her temper with his handsome tanned face, his white broken teeth, his thick stupid curls, his foreign problems, the swamp of his need, sucking down tea and coffee and kindness, the scruples that stopped him making love to her, his pallid, boneless daughter and grey hopeless wife, the way he'd made her husband cross with her.

He looked shocked. "Not to shout, Mary. I am sensitive, like you. I am artist. Not to shout." He looked as though he was going to cry.

"Isaac, I'll make you some tea. But you must get the job done. Find some of your friends. People to help you. Between you you'll get the job done. Won't you?"

He shrugged. "OK, I promise." But he drank his tea and went, hardly speaking to her. "Tomorrow I am here with friend early."

He rang on the door at seven thirty, half an hour earlier than ever before. Edward had just left for the office and she was bleary and vague, in a hastily donned jade silk kimono. Isaac's eyes ran automatically over her body, but his mouth was a line, and his eyes were bloodshot. "Daughter very sick last night," he said. "Van is no good again. And I haven't car, because wife must have it to visit hospital. Mary, you will drive me."

"Drive you where?"

"Drive me to find men."

"Your friends? Why can't they drive themselves?"

"But the friends, it turned out, were out of commission. One genius was working in south London, another was having "surge" on his spine, another had gone back home, which was dangerous. "Maybe he die," Isaac muttered.

"So what are you going to do?" she screamed at him, impatient with his broken stories. Why hadn't they got a proper builder? Why was her husband mean, why was she feeble?

Isaac was frightened of this new savage woman, so different from the mild, flirtatious one he knew. "Please, Mary. I know where we find men. But quick, drive me now, please."

"I'm not dressed,' she said. Not that she often did get completely dressed, nowadays. And rarely put shoes on, for there wasn't any reason. Mary hadn't driven the car for some time. Why should she go out? Most days Isaac came in. She shopped on-line, and friends came to her, not so many as before, but enough, surely. (They tended to bring bulging yellow packets of photographs, tall glowing children and gummy grandchildren. She hadn't any children, so she couldn't compete. She didn't want to know about other people's babies.) "Mary, put on clothes now," he insisted. It was exciting to her to have Isaac tell her something so directly, and she went off upstairs without protesting, returning dressed in the first thing she found in her cupboard, a smart Chanel-copy suit with gold buttons and pink braid.

He looked at her strangely as he opened the car door, but he bowed slightly, and she felt exalted, though the car looked like an old cast-up shark, grey and discoloured and rattling with teeth.

On the way to wherever it was they were going she kept sneaking glances at Isaac's profile, his long tanned jaw, his sad male lips, talking, talking about his daughter. Nice to be driven by a handsome man. She was excited: it was an outing. She didn't listen to what he was saying.

The car slowed down in the northern suburbs. "Here we find men," Isaac said. His mobile rang and he swore and dived for it, retrieving the steering-wheel at the last. As the traffic waited at a bottleneck, he listened intently, then shouted at the phone, finally clicking it off after an explosion of furious consonants. Mary was surprised to see tears in his eyes.

"Are you all right, Isaac?" she asked him, tentative.

"Yes, Mary. Now I do work."

"But you're crying, Isaac."

"Is only dust."

"Oh. That's good."

Her attention was distracted. They were driving towards a long desolate road, straight, running between Victorian terraces, but there was something in front of the terraces, something that at first she mis-saw as trees, grey shapeless trees with aimless branches, one or two hundred metres of trees, something that struck her as strange in a city, but then she realised they were not trees. They were thickets of men, standing in clumps, mostly silent, staring at the traffic, men in rough clothes with worn brown skin, men looking furtive, men looking hungry, men with no colour beneath their tan. Dozens of them. Scores. Hundreds? Not a single woman among those thin faces. Washed out tracksuits, ill-fitting trousers. Some of their hair was white with dust. Most of them were smoking lethargically. The slogans on their chests looked tired, dated.

"What is it, Isaac? What's going on?"

"Here we find men. Stop car. I do it."

"I don't want these people!" she found herself shouting. They looked ill and strange, not exotic like Isaac. Scenting interest, some had turned towards the car, were raising their hands to attract attention. Some were calling out, but she couldn't understand them. Then she caught some broken English: "Only fifty!" "Only forty!" She felt naked and stupid in her pink Chanel ribbons and terrible glittering golden buttons.

"Not to shout, Mary." He looked very weary. "Is OK. You leave to me."

"They're not coming in my house. I want proper workmen."

"Is workmen, Mary" His phone rang again. He cursed, and threw it down on the back seat, got out of the car and left her alone.

On the pavement, Isaac started talking to people. She sat inside trembling, clutching the steering wheel. What if they suddenly rushed the car, snatched her handbag, raped her, mugged her? The phone rang again, urgent, painful. After thirteen rings she picked it up. A woman's voice shouted in an unknown language. "I don't understand," Mary whispered. The woman's cries became more desperate. "I don't understand. Speak English, please," Mary said. "You're in England. Please speak English."

She felt better as she said it, briefly, in this unfamiliar place, that had no rules; she stood up for something she thought she believed in, but then the phone went silent, dead, and she laid it on the seat, and felt worse than ever. It must have been his wife. She spoke no English.

Isaac came back with three hangdog giants. They got into the back without speaking a word. There was a smell of metal, and old cigarette smoke, and something acrid, unspeakable.

"I think your wife phoned," she said to Isaac. She was powerless: whatever would happen, would happen.

He shrugged. He would not look at her. "Drive home please, Mary. We finish the painting."

The cloud had cleared by the time they got back, and the sun drilled through, fiercely hot. That long dark road with its unhealthy armies had left her a spreading weight of terror. Isaac had come to her on false pretences; he had let her imagine him framed by blue mountains, aromatic meadows, sturdy flocks, but now she saw he just came from this, a sour sad place where no one was happy.

They worked all day, the three strangers and Isaac. She heard him shout at them from time to time. She went out twice, nervously, to see what they were doing, and offer tea, but Isaac refused, waving one hand in dismissal, going on painting with the other one. She felt unsettled, sitting bowed in her study, trying to invent a love story, safe in her room in the cool pleasant house but uneasily aware of the four male bodies crawling all over it, obsessed, intent, locked to her hot surfaces, sweating, grunting.

Isaac came in once, to ask her for money, five times what she would normally pay him. These men were apparently very expensive. "I haven't got it," she said, indignant. She only kept enough cash to pay Isaac. "You go to the bank, Mary, find money. All finish today," he said, darkly. She drove to the bank, and it felt almost normal, though the unfamiliar shoes hurt her toes and ankles. She started to feel better once she held the money. Such a thick, crisp packet, and it came so easily, warm from the machine on the sun-baked wall, where everything was as it should be.

The men stayed till seven, and then filed in, burnt red by the sun, their hair splashed with white, their lips grey-coated, not meeting her eyes. They looked hardly human. She went out and inspected. The job was finished. Isaac spoke to the others, and they went to the car, without saying goodbye, as if Mary herself hardly existed.

She needed Isaac to smile at her. "Would you like a drink, Isaac?" she pleaded. "You must be thirsty after all that work. While I put the money in an envelope."

"No thank you, Mary. Men wait in car."

"Oh, they'll be all right. They'll be perfectly happy."

"No thank you, Mary. I go now, please."

When Edward arrived, they had just driven away. He was itching for a fight: the train was hellish, boiling. "Did he bloody well turn up?" he came in shouting.

"Go and have a look," said her voice from the study.

Five minutes later, he came in, smiling, knocked at her door, saw her sitting there. "At long last,' he said. 'Doesn't look too bad. And he's finally cleared all his paint-pots away. The whole bloody lot. Why are you crying?"

In November, some tiles blew off the roof, and Edward told her to telephone Isaac. She had missed him, sharply, day by day. Once she was forced to go out to the dentist and saw a man exactly like him, but older, walking down a high street in another part of London, hunched over a pram, its handle hung about with shopping. Obviously though, it wasn't really Isaac. He wasn't the sort of man you saw with a pram. Now she tried his number; it was still unobtainable. Edward seemed to have forgotten the roof, but then there was a storm and more tiles came down. "For God's sake, woman," he said to her. "You haven't got a proper job, can't you find a workman?" She rang the number repeatedly, weeping.

Next day she got dressed as soon as Edward was gone and drove to the suburbs, remembering. Isaac's sweet dark eyes, the slight roughness on his jaw. He had opened doors for her. Surely he liked her. He gave her a rose. He – admired her.

The forest of men was there, as before. She kept nearly stopping, was afraid, drove on, and finally drew up beside a couple of men. "I need only one man, she said, firmly. They looked at each other, and bargained, briefly. They seemed very cheap, half what Isaac was charging her.

The man she took had black eyes like Isaac. He was young, and slight, with a thin clever face, and the tee-shirt he wore was a plain dark red. Perhaps he came from the same country as Isaac. She thought his mouth was quite appealing.

At twelve o'clock she called him in for coffee. "Thirsty on the roof," she said, kindly, with elaborate mime to help things along. "I understand you," he said. "It's OK. Nearly everything, I understand. In my own country, I learned good English. I am a student. I *was* a student . . ." (Yes, she thought, they are all students. The mini-cab drivers all claimed to be students.) ". . . sixteenth and seventeenth century history . . ." He started to talk about invasions, displacements. Oh dear, she thought, he may be a bore.

"Where are you from?" she cut in. He told her.

"My last man came from there," she said. She felt a rush of hope and pleasure. She told him the name. "Perhaps you know him. Very hard workers, your countrymen."

His face had changed. It was charged with interest. "But Isaac is a great man," he said.

"Excellent worker," she agreed.

"Is a great artist," he said.

She laughed. It was charming, how they all praised each other. Every single one was a genius.

"No, really," he said. "He is an artist. We think he is a genius."

"Yes, Isaac liked to think he was an artist. That's why we got on. I am artistic, too."

"In my country, Isaac is a very great artist. Abroad you don't know him, but in my country . . . But now I think he says he will do no more painting."

She wasn't sure she had understood him. For a moment she'd thought he meant actual art. "Yes, he's stopped working for me, since the summer," she said. "That's why we need a new man, really."

She went to the kitchen to fetch some biscuits. He carried on talking in the rich, empty room. "Isaac says he will do no more painting. Is a great loss for my country. He says life is over, since his daughter died. His beautiful daughter died, in August."

The packet wouldn't open; she was wrenching it, noisily, crashing bourbon biscuits on to bone china, but she managed to pick out the single word "daughter", and remembered Isaac's wife, her misery, the apples she ate, her grey distance. The wife and daughter had spoiled it all. "Are you married?" she called back through from the kitchen.

He shook his head. "Life is too hard to marry," he said. "Life is beautiful, but life is short."

"I see you are sensitive," she said, "like me. I am an artist, you know. I write. There will be other jobs for you," she said, smiling.

To Effervesce

Charles Buchan

A) is for *Arnaud*, which is, in point of fact, my name.

B) is for *breathe*. I must tell you that I find it hard sometimes.

- I have a little attic room in Haringey; small fanlights look like catseyes in the slanted ceiling, not quite closing, because, the landlord tells me, staggering up the stairs (wheezing all the way) from his sweet shop below, wearing a broad brown apron that I have never seen clean, tells me, I tell you, in broken English (his, not mine, as he is Turkish and I am only French, and besides I am taking a class), that there is subsidence, movement in the building. So the windows let in a slim and whistling breeze, and the cheap paper lantern swings in a disgruntled circle. And my door drags against the threadbare carpet at its hinge end, like a child dragging its feet, and at the other end stands a full three inches from the floor. And for this, for this I pay more than is reasonable for London, let alone Paris or my own city of Nîmes. Mehmet shrugs his work-weary, round shoulders; he thinks there is some kind of ahistorical *entente* between France and Turkey that will make amends for all of his shortcomings; diplomacy is no easy art, I understand.

C) is for *Career*.

- Or lack thereof. Well, I am a waiter on certain days, and it is a truly great thing to sidle up to wealthy people, dangle one's wrists, and look haughty. And afterwards, Ramon and I, we go to Camden Lock, smoke a little something, and his eyes narrow faster than mine, so that he is transformed suddenly into some kind of archetypal Chinaman from *Tintin*. Ramon inevitably gets talking to somebody from somewhere, Jason from Atlanta, or Sophia who studies at an institute, and who, to catch her outbound flight, had to drive through Grozny, and, *my God*, the things she has seen and endured (pulling her allegedly real fur about her, although it is July), mean that she needs a smoke now and again to ease her mind. Ramon called her a *fake sheikh*, which is something I think he read in a newspaper, something I found hysterical at the time, though I fail to understand it – then, as now. And every time we go for marijuana, Ramon and I make vows, and he takes it very seriously, his face becoming sombre and inscrutable, and it has the feel of a ritual within our control, profound yet soothing. We vow firstly to get new and better-paid jobs, as minions in coffee shops or in *Prêt à Manger*; we vow also to kill our boss, who is the embodiment of evil, and very conscious of the impression that she makes on people of more importance than herself, and wholly ignorant of the fact that everyone beneath her will always want to kill her. And I heard her tell Markus, the head waiter, that I could *bugger off back to Paris on the next Eurostar* if my serving skills were not honed *prontissimo*. (Mind you, on what they pay she should know that I'd only be able to cross the *Tunnel sous la Manche* on foot). And we try to vow more, and often partly get there, before we giggle like children, because that is exactly what we are: we are children laughing nervously at something we do not wholly comprehend, wanting, as we do, to live as grown-ups in a country not native to us.

D) is for *dilution*.

- Because, and this is my philosophy, a part of oneself dies abroad, and one is eternally in search of it. Or maybe it is like being the child of a divorce between one country and another, the stranger parent having got custody.

Once, I even dragged my agnostic self into the French Catholic church off Leicester Square (beside that cheap cinema, you know it), and, annoyingly, as it was Eastertime, I had to sit through eight Stations of the Cross before I could escape. The dilution is a gentle poisoning, oddly corroding what it is that one holds very dearly familiar in one's mind, until all that matters is the daily round of work, a drink with a diluted friend, and then sleep. I find myself, therefore, sympathizing with the Palestinian asylum-seeker I meet in a bar (oh, the thrill of going out on one's own) who screeches at me for forty-seven minutes about Israeli atrocities, before she asks to borrow the fare for the night bus 'home', suddenly enunciating with a pristine clarity that her earlier words had missed. It is not that I am unsympathetic; it is just that the dilution is a solitary thing, you know, even if an Irishman will find consolation in his emerald-decor pub, whether in California or Zanzibar: what he feels he might be missing is his sensation alone.

E) is for *effervescence.*

• When I came here, I gave up the body. Not in some kind of Sufistic way, although there is a man not far from my *atelier* who can promise to deliver this, if it interests you. I saw his card in the newsagents' window. No, I just make use of the body, for what it's worth. There is a photograph on a web page, with an email address, and the men that like the picture send in a message, messages that I retrieve in an EasyEverything near the restaurant on Oxford Street, and I meet them in the evenings, money up front (I've been had before), and they climb up the six flights of cold stairs to the room where my lantern hovers dubiously, and then they fuck me.

- It is the congestion, I think, the constant actual *embouteillage* sensation of London that brought me to it. You would say a traffic jam, but the French is almost better, the notion of a blockage, a bottled-up way of living. Ramon and I sway towards Mornington Crescent tube (we had forgotten about Camden, our minds being quite devoid of sense), like people who have arrived at their holiday destination and unpacked their cases: we have let go. On the tube we swelter in shocking proximity, tall Ramon beaming down upon me, his eyes still smiling. All the other people hold their bags close, their eyes darting around suspiciously, cutting away if they catch someone else's, determined to remain anonymous. The hostility is a suffocating embrace, a sort of harsh matronly English love that travelled with someone's nanny on a steam train from the provinces to arrive at Paddington at least eight decades before now, weatherproof and alteration-resistant. The ravens have not left the Tower, either. And this cold race, adoptive choice of many, with its confused tradition of superiority over, and accommodation of, other peoples, its determination always to maintain a frosty civility (as if forever semi-detached from the world at large), this race will not permit itself, even inside this oppressive tube, a moment, one unrestrained moment: a collective dropping of the guard. Instead, mouths frowning and brows knitting, everybody waits for a later privacy in which to peel off the accumulated layers of silt and mire, moral and actual, uncork themselves and effervesce. I see it in the faces of the men, and read it in what they choose not to reveal.

F) is for *fromage frais*. You British have it all wrong.

G) is for *Georgios*.

- Adonis Karagiorgos lives in the room below mine, and works nights (thankfully). Mehmet is particularly mean to him, because poor Georgios has some kind of hang-up about arguing with a Turk, even in a badly lit room too close to the railway line for comfortable sleep; also, Mehmet always calls him Adonis, too, just to embarrass, as Georgios has possibly the worst skin ever, walks with a limp and talks with a stammer. I like him very much, think of him as avuncular: on his thirty-first birthday, we went for dim sum in Chinatown. Sometimes we cross on the stairs, until someone told us it was bad luck, so now we always reverse our steps, and yell updates at each other as to where we are standing.

H) is for *happiness.*

I) for *illegalities.*

- About which I know nothing, although I got seriously cross-questioned at Heathrow (I forget which terminal), as *illegals* are very much to be found out and sent packing; then, the British Embassy lost my passport when I was applying for residency, and I had to buy a new French one, and the following day this Very Posh Voice telephoned, and Georgios answered, bleary-eyed at ten in the morning, and later he told me that they had relocated my original passport, which was so *i*rritating that it *i*rked *i*ntently, although later Mathieu, who works at the Ritz and lives off the tips, took me for a near-authentic *café au lait* in South Kensington, which is Francophile enough briefly to reconcile me to the expense of this city, this snobbish city that, as night falls, is my undoing, as people misinterpret my dark face (my Senegalese inheritance), and (*i*) steel themselves for violence, as I am surely black enough to want to attack them; (*ii*) prepare to say no in the event of my asking for spare change or offering to sell them something *i*llicit; (*iii*) quicken their pace noticeably, in an attempt to quicken their pace without its appearing noticeable.

J/K/L/M/N/O: "Just Kidding," Laughed Mehmet, "Nice Outfit."

- Mathieu, like one in six gay men in London, is HIV positive, and, unlike them, also has a greatly supportive girlfriend, Ariadne, who is part-Algerian and has perfect French. They are getting married next March. As a favour, he asked me, when a little unwell, to escort her to a plush function held by the company that she works for, some big accountancy firm.
- But I don't have anything to wear, I say, and he goes, I'll lend you mine, and I say, Your What?, and he goes, It's Black Tie, and I go, Will it Fit?, and he thinks it might need a belt.
- At a round table, over which Ariadne presides looking like some demure yet glamorous Egyptian empress, calmly authoritative, I am sitting silently, trying not to betray my true self in spite of a mad desire to assist the serving staff. For the accountants assembled, it is enough that I am French, however, and I do not have to explain that the stand-in Mathieu works in a bar, paying for his medication using Ariadne's earnings. I am exotic enough already. The accountants, strange breed, wax lyrical: finewine*painauchocolat*ArcdeTriompheDepardieu. Funny, I never thought of myself as some kind of emissary, that I should hear all this and consider it praise; it's not as if *les rosbifs* all quote Shakespeare and look like Princess Anne. I need Ramon's remedy, a quick spliff.
- Earlier, I struggle down six flights into Mehmet's spotless shop, where his son is arranging some trays to showcase some fresh baklava. Mehmet, smoking a Camel Light in the corner, and licking the occasional chubby finger to turn the page of an old *Olay* newspaper, rises with comic speed out of his chair, about to launch a most benevolent proprietorial smile. Then he recognizes me, although his bushy, greying eyebrows suggest

incredulity. It is really you, he says after a while, still sounding doubtful. I signal that I need his help; I've not tied a bow tie before. He labours each step of the way up to my collar, fumbles around, cigarette in peril on his lower lip. After his big, dry fingers finish, he takes a sweeping step back, looks me up and down, crinkles his forehead, and scratches his temples. Dreadful, he pronounces, to my dismay. (What would Mathieu say?) Then he laughs, and his laugh becomes a splutter, a throaty cough. "Just kidding," he says, eventually, finding his voice again, "Nice outfit."

(Where I last was is where I am now from; the lazy solution, when people ask. Thus, Golders Green, Barons Court, Queen's Park, Archway, all provide answers that eliminate further questions. P stands for *provenance*, something that grows indistinct or simply solidifies, forming an indestructible core within me, allowing for a second identity to be grafted on, that of Londoner: cosmopolitan to the point of standoffish, or else brusque.

I split a smile with Mathieu when, after a beautiful piece of theatre, three Arabic businessmen finish their mathematics, work out their bill in *JDs*, Jordanian Dollars. The process of being uprooted is never fully accomplished, I deduce, a feeling that becomes more pronounced on the nights when I see Aleksandr, a stoical Russian with the loneliest, most fragile porcelain face, who transports the scars of his military service years everywhere.)

- Q, for *quixotic*, as Ramon has this idea that we, the waiters, should throw down our cutlery and go on strike. Georgios, who works nights in a vitamin factory, says his guys started a walk-out or a sit-in (something that sounded as if it did not involve too much effort, actually), and Ramon, off his face as usual – all of us joked that he'll be discovered one day in a coma in a dodgy smack den in, say, Clapham – got all excited, and remembered his course at Birkbeck (or "How He Got To Be Here In The First Place"), and earnestly appealed to me to participate in his fervour. Mehmet, however, waddling over to say that he would have to close in ten minutes, burst the illusory bubble: he asked, Did we really stand a chance of negotiating a pay rise? At which Ramon, who faithfully sends money back each month to Lima for his sister and her son, cried and cried and cried, until even Mehmet softened a little, and made more coffee voluntarily, and, in spite of being more tetchy than usual since Ramadan, went so far as to offer, the next time he goes to the mosque at Finsbury Park, to speak to his cousin – who runs a Thomas Cook – about holding a cheap flight for him (it's been three years, almost), which made me think, really, Mehmet, he is not so bad.

(R is for Royalty)

- I had been sceptical about the strike action, and Ramon had looked daggers at me, sure, but even he sympathized when I got to serve this Major and his five equine children, which was mission impossible, and really beyond my usual job of writing the orders in big capital letters for the serial murder chef who has tattoos and lives in Hainault, my usual job of looking vacant and sounding distinctly foreign as I explain what a *vichyssoise* entails. Ramon was sympathetic enough to convey with a glance that later we would smoke our way out of it, and, as their voices ruled the room, and the Major clicked his fingers to summon me, and I experienced this urge to blowtorch the entire family to death for behaving like royalty, *tout soudain* it came to me – "My London Epiphany" – that tradition and pomp and ceremony and ostentatious display were somehow less offensive here (no guillotine); that the English humour was at once an indulgence and a mockery of peacocks, court and fanfare; that to forbear was consistent with the *embouteillage*: how easy it is not to complain, and just get on with it, stiff upper lip *et al.*

- So I forbore, fairly winning the Major over, or at least earning just the most absurd tip, and I felt quite contrary afterwards, as if I had been begging for this commission *(S is for Supplicant)*, as if all the time I had been imploring at his feet in my grubby poverty, entreating some small favour, making a temporary false idol of an ordinary person that had attracted attention.

  Afterwards we called Mathieu, who was seeing a specialist on Harley Street, and I went to meet him there alone (Ramon had disappeared, his ache for cigarettes unrelenting), and stood gingerly in the reception of a smart clinic or *practice*, full of fear and only a little hope, both futile emotions in fact as he said nothing when we left, nothing until we had sat down on a bench in a small square, nothing at all until he said (perhaps only to assuage), I'm not so bad. I didn't know how to answer, how to read his remark, and looked blankly into his piercing, sad grey eyes. He met my gaze, his mood changing. He said, How are you? And in his sudden anger, he almost spat; something had to be wrong. And I'm still not sure whether it was out of a frustrated sense of curiosity or the concern of love, but then he said, What is really going on with you?

T) is for *truth*.

- "I borrowed the room deposit from Ramon, and the job is only part-time, and I don't have the fees for the next class at the uninviting college above a shop on Tottenham Court Road, and I sell my body, and I miss home but I can't go back." And I've got this far.

U) is for *untruth.*

- "Yes, Maman, I teach now, I have some students learning French. The room is great, I've decorated. You should maybe come visit, but it's expensive . . . yes, *vachement bien,* really. Mathieu's great too, never been better." *Je suis un vrai menteur.*

V), for *violence.*

- It's a strange dream. The restaurant is open, but empty. I can see a lollipop lady outside, which is a bit unusual for this part of town. I am in my uniform, which is scuffed and ripped, and my sleeves are rolled up almost to my elbows, and blood from self-inflicted cuts runs thickly down my arms, and I tear at the skin, spill the liquid into glasses and over plates, staining the table cloth, dabbing at the mess with the napkins, falling into a chair as my left leg trips my right. And the room begins to thump, as if it is a club at night pulsating with music, and suddenly I've left the room, and the table buffet is all ready made, the same table laden with blood and body parts cut up, broken or dismembered: *I've made a meal of it.*
- You were screaming, says Georgios, handing me my inhaler as I feel for my throat, You woke me up. But he does not sound too resentful, mercifully; it is the weekend, after all. He looks at me, briefly concerned, then smiles. You're all right, he says, you'll be fine.

Fyndet
(or: I Kan Eat Anyone)

Iain Sinclair

The swish and swoosh of sea/traffic, just below the level of nuisance. The window that didn't close. Kaporal couldn't unpick the acoustic weave. Nightcars, tankers. The long, steady race of the sea against an exposed bridge of rock that would be covered by morning. Seen only by vagrants, beach drinkers. Like a tender migraine, it came in waves. The news of his mortality. He sweated, tossed. Rucking the nylon sheet, exposing thin knees. Dirty muslin across the window hole: a fault in his eye. Soft lens left overnight in a dish of sour milk.

He slept, he didn't sleep. The siren of a police car, an ambulance. A ship hooting in the channel. Dream sprockets, flight. Headbutting a stranger, living in a stone boat. This was true. Truer than the rest. The Londoner existed, on sufferance, in marine exile. By an ever-changing shore. By the privilege of water. The reflected dazzle of the sea came early, through the muslin. Fires of driftwood, broken furniture, newspaper. On a slip of sharp stones. Men with cans of strong lager. Creatures who inhabited the cavernous spaces under the promenade. He would join them later, keep his distance. Listen to the monologues.

Now the gulls were active, the brilliance of the day couldn't be held back. It was too early to make his call. He'd have to wait for hours, until the waves of unconsciousness rolled back, cleared like morning mist. Until London woke up. This *was* London. As he had known it. This was where London had shifted. Where asylum seekers stopped seeking. The ones who had been persuaded to sign away that part of it, the quest for some form of official recognition. They walked. They paced. They gestured. Sallow skins with the sun bleached out of them by daily increments. Occupied with their own strategies, they ignored the native memory men. Former citizens. Of Tottenham and Finsbury. The men from the Balkans were on the pavements at dawn, outside the locked doors of the relevant agencies. They hung about, waiting for the van, in a street of good houses that had recently gone under. The work was there – if you were willing. Cheap trainers and yellow hard-hats (returned at the day's end).

After they dispersed, Kaporal was among his own kind. The banished. Transported sex offenders. Charity shop casuals. The ones who marched too vigorously up the middle of the pavement; undeviating, muttering to themselves. Scrawny kids in twos and threes scouting the play of human traffic in a sidestreet minimart. No cash is left overnight on these premises. Hackney-on-Sea. Twinned with Tirana.

Can't fail.

His victim, the man on the other end of the phone, was bored. The yawn carried across the river, the motorway, the Downs. Hissing over the sixty-odd miles from London. Kaporal could hear that angular kettle coming to the boil. He could imagine his last professional contact, back in the Smoke, above the van hire yard, scratching, leaning back in an orthopaedic chair. Picking up a book. A review copy. Wondering how long he'd let this maniac run before he faked a call on the other line, an Irishman at the door. Builder, postman.

You've been out there. You've seen them. Kaporal said. Saturday families. Men with no previous . . . Ever-so-slightly pregnant women. Sperm still wriggling in their knickers as they haul the poor sods into the Mondeo, head off down the A13, and . . .

They tell me the meatballs are rather good.

The potential favour-granter, that jaded metropolitan, who was balancing the slim black phone between cheek and shoulder, couldn't help himself. He had a child somewhere in the suburbs. He remembered those outings. The lunches. There was always a driving range in the vicinity. A chalk quarry. What had they *done* with all that chalk? Was it still used? Blackboards. Today's special. Swedish meatballs.

Have you considered the books? he said.

Kaporal's interruption wasn't altogether unwelcome. The London writer had come to a stop. The desk was too wide for his narrative. He'd been gazing out of the window at the indiscriminate sprawl of Crouch End. Wondering why it played so much better than it sounded. Fine gradations of light, on muck and slate and brick, on soft greenery. He was about to ring around the usual names. Trawling for gossip, exploitable anecdotes.

Why is it that the only books on those patinated pine shelves, fantasy offices and pretend sitting-rooms, are by Patricia Highsmith? (The man continued while hungry Kaporal chewed on his tongue.) One title: *Fyndet*. Highsmith in Swedish. Dozens and dozens of mint copies. Multiples. Unread and never likely to be read. Do you ever think about that? An eliminated novel. They could have produced fake books or bought in ballast from Hay-on-Wye. But they decided that Highsmith was exactly right, as décor. A Renoir on the cover. A fat chocolate-box nude. *La Dormeuse*. I've never been able to get past the Highsmiths. I'm still standing there, at the top of the stairs, in the first chamber, when I get a whiff of the meatballs. I'm sure they pump scent through the ventilation ducts to keep you going. Otherwise, you'd turn on your heel and walk straight out.

That's my point. You've got it.

What? Simplify shopping by carrying single titles by a single author?

A guide. A book that explains how it works. A map. Like the *A–Z*. Like having a personal shopper to talk you through the various zones. Nobody, nobody ever knows where they're going. Or if they'll manage to find a way out. Existential terror in their faces. They anticipate the queue as soon as they pick up one of those empty blue bags. They're intimidated by size. They *have* to be filled. It's compulsory. What they want is a colour-coded pocket guide to the mysteries of the off-highway retail world. Where to browse, where to chill. The secret alcoves, hidden corners. You're never going to get out alive without my chart. Nothing works. The TV sets don't play and you can't buy them. The sound-systems are mute. The computers aren't connected. Books aren't for reading. The punters have to be told. They need it explained: what's real, what's for sale, what you can take home. Bright yellow letters on washable blue laminate. *Find It. I Know Every Aisle.* Kaporal's Guide to the Lakeside Labyrinth.

Great. Great idea. Tell me how it goes. Dentist's appointment. Just remembered. Sorry.

You're in on it. I need you to punt this, talk it up. A percentage on every copy. Cheque in the post. Never leave Claremont Road. The web site's already in place. Professional bitchers and complainers have set it up. It can't, can't miss. I'm going there today. I'll give you a call, an update from Essex.

From her unblemished window, Lucy looked out on – what? A future lake? A misconceived water-feature that was visibly silting up, as she watched it; as she stood, perfectly still, left hand gripping the glossy-sticky ledge, smoking. In a dressing-gown she didn't recognize. A tartan dressing-gown that was too short in the sleeve and that smelt, annoyingly, of butter. There were, she discovered, crumbs in the pocket.

Plastic rubbish floated on a quilt of green scum: before the site had been declared officially open. If you could open a worked-out chalk quarry. As anything other than a suicide pit. Everything was new. Everything was unreal, uninitiated. A principality of the repossessed: she saw other women. In the dead-end crescents, the cancelled avenues. She saw children too young to be recognized as discrete entities. She noticed a curious absence of dogs. There were no men. She witnessed hinterlands where new roads ran out, lines of slender lighting-poles diminishing into unconvinced nothingness. Neither town nor country. Cars abandoned on wide verges, torched, engines exposed. Blocks of mint new houses imposed on territory that had not yet been introduced to the notion of compromise. There was a certain frisson – her hand slid through the overlap of her dressing-gown – in lodging (nobody *lived* here yet) in the gap between the virtual and the actual. She could see the lights of the traffic, outlining the arch of the invisible suspension bridge. Cars in the clouds.

Her fingers moved to the rhythm of the road, that remote abstraction. It did not touch her. Later, perhaps, she would walk to the quarry, look down on dark water, the scrub, the impenetrable thickets, while she contemplated . . .

Pig ignorance, stupidity, fools trapped within the unstoppable processes of their lumbering, awkward bodies. And happy to be so. Volunteers for oblivion. The striped rugby shirts of men too fat to haul themselves, unaided, out of their 4-wheel drives. Thick white trainers of the untrained. Ironed sportswear. Watches, bracelets. Catalogue mufti in which to pretend they are somewhere else. In which to pretend that they know where they're going. Discriminations of the indiscriminate. Estuarine Essex on parole, loosed in trash bazaars.

Kaporal, limping after his three-day trek from the coast, had penetrated the big blue warehouse. The horror. Was it a storage facility or a retail outlet? Did you make purchases or were you, simply, brought here to admire? To walk yourself into exhaustion, a healthy appetite for those gravy-glazed meatballs, simmering in their metallic trays?

It was worse than he had imagined. (You can't imagine endlessness.) These places existed, so Kaporal affirmed, to facilitate divorce. The women were all permanently ten minutes pregnant. And happy about it. They knew what to do, they had a shopping list (and a mother, a sister). Kaporal had none of these. He'd mislaid them. The warehouse woman were child-bearing, but trim with it. They weren't pregnant all over. They were in that interesting condition achieved by females in soap operas, a cushion of foam stuffed up the jumper. Gym-taut in other respects, groomed. Incapable of sweating.

Kaporal sweated in the artificial twilight, a moth with foreknowledge of extinction. This dole of yellow electricity, evenly distributed, troubled him. The guide book scam was never going to work. It was impossible. His papers had been stamped. Status confirmed: recidivist bachelor. Serial offender. He'd never got far enough into a relationship to bring one of his wives out here. By the time he remembered where he lived, they'd gone. Decamped with a financial adviser, a painter and decorator. He was a wounded solitary. He stood out, among the forests of shaved pine, the primary colour plastics, a pariah.

Other men acquired the knack of pretending not to be in Thurrock, not entirely. They brandished mobiles, talked loudly, as if they were still on the street, fishing the quarry. At a football match. In the office. They made their contribution to the general noise, the acoustic rubble that held London together, fizzing interference between photovoltaic scanners. Spit in a dish. London had leaked into the brownfield swamps, trickled out from the centre like scum from a punctured sewage pipe.

I dream: roads. Said Kaporal. Loud enough to draw attention to himself. But not loud enough to stop the flow, the surge, the blocked aisles. Lost families with their huge, empty bags. This was anti-shopping. A hard lesson learnt in how to undo retail therapy. The warehouse was an exercise in exploded topography. Flat-earthing. Creationism for beginners. There is no evolution. Everything stays the same forever. Everything is written, fated. The warehouse was a flat-packed Lutheran conspiracy.

Foot hard on the pedal, Kaporal insisted. I dream. And the landscape dreams with me.

I dreamt last night Lucy said to a friend she hadn't seen for five was it eight years. Dreamt.

No not about the cat again tell me it's not.

No no I . . . Please. Well it *was* strange, a sleeping-bag. With pedals. I floated over the ramp and onto the bridge and off along the river and out to sea. And when I came back home to my old home in town there was a man in the house at my kitchen table and he was gutting a huge rabbit a hare he said it was. Wearing a butcher's thing a riding mac smeared with blood and nothing else. Roadkill. His arm disappeared into it the animal and he followed. The hare was a glove I've got to go new place completely bare I don't have a stick of furniture, curtains cushions chairs. No soap no carpet. I've been through the catalogue you can't order on the phone and they don't deliver.

Do you have a car?

Not in years not since but now I'll have to take the plunge I've been looking down on that place from the top of the quarry nowhere else to walk. Mecca. Forbidden city. Forbidden to unbelievers. Glass towers domes minarets I'll wear the burkha. All cars around here thousands and thousands in gleaming paddocks curves side-mirrors windshields and chrome. Not for sale, export. Hard light glinting from pebbles. at night it's different, red pulse in the window. A burkha or a Burberry. Ships at sea. Warnings. Lost sailors.

You can't map the unmappable. I don't know if I'm still at the start or if I've managed to sneak in through the backdoor.

Kaporal, though he peddled facts for a living (printouts, quotes, transcripts, semi-official paper), didn't like them. Wasn't comfortable. Couldn't hold them between his teeth.

Kept his face stuffed in a bun to avoid the consequences of his profession: having to say what he'd seen, replaying the past for some interested investor. Patrons paid him to avoid experiences better performed by a surrogate.

When words came out of a machine, hardcopy, they had a certain conviction. By night, in the dark. Out there in an estate, somewhere south of the river. On the marshes. Different marshes. On the edge of a storage zone. Anonymous block buildings, windowless, in tin or concrete. Numbered units: they're not mapped, not listed. Maps can't keep up. You'll never find the same boulevard twice.

He couldn't remember, drink taken. E-rith. E-rith, he thinks they said. Someone said. Erith. The last night before he came over the water, in transit to Thurrock, talking the gig through with chums, with Rory and Stefan, he nearly had it. A couple of bottles, a camera, TV on. Blue light. And he recognized, four or five hours in, that they were actually in *different* rooms. Talking to themselves. Rory alongside the TV. Stefan upstairs on the bed with the guitar. Kaporal in the kitchen, fridge open. Opening then shutting the fridge door to see if he could figure out if the light stayed on all the time or if it were somehow triggered by the movement of the door, his action. And each time it opened he ate a forfeit, an olive or an onion, a sardine that had slipped into the salad tray.

All of them in separate rooms. All of them talking. Wonderful riffs unheard. Kaporal with the digicam, shooting his feet the floor, peering into rooms. Drinking. Vodka and cold coffee. Pissing on his shoes.

Basically, they all wanted to confess. And no one was prepared, or qualified, to be the confessor. The man in the shadows. Granter of absolution. Rory did. Confess. Stefan was messing about with chords and Kaporal was up and down the stairs, detouring to the kitchen, checking the fridge, running the tap, drinking water, drinking and sweating. No curtains drawn. They didn't have curtains. You could look in from outside. Every light in the house.

Rory was vaguely connected, cousin to cousin, to the royals. He had a standing invite to the Queen Mum's obsequies, the Abbey. He'd had it for years. He said he knew he'd heard at a dinner party Di was pregnant. Confirmed by a French quack the ring bought the day of the night in the tunnel the crash. And Stefan who hadn't actually so far as Kaporal could remember achieved *anything* by way of a coherent sentence all evening he was jamming and singing bits and laughing said: You keep going on about how everything around the motorway goes back to M16 – Noye, Swanley, alien invasion, traffic, pollution. The one thing that doesn't is the royals. Have you ever seen one of them on the M25? They go *under* it, on the way out, flag-draped coffin. But they never ever ever travel *on* it. Now why is that? I have the TV day and night you have to out here it's the only way of staying in the weave.

Why do you? Kaporal said. Live out here. And anyway whose house is this? Rory or Stefan? Are you both queer all the time?

Listen. Stefan said. Listen to me. Why is it that royals never go on the M25? It's forbidden. In the rules. Hereditary. Hundreds of thousands of years. (They laughed.) Flowers chucked under the wheels of the black limo. The only time they see the motorway, looking up out of the coffin at a flyover, Junction 15, or the bridge on the Colnbrook by-pass if they use the old road. They have to be dead. It's in the regulations.

And another thing. He continued, much later, first light. M25 is the dyslexic way of saying M16, the code. Once you've cracked that you've got the picture, man. Same with politicians, they never use it. Never have. Thatcher didn't even drive a hundred yards when she opened the bugger. Frit of snipers, IRA. Snips the ribbon, shifts a cone and off.

Motorcade through the suburbs, Borehamwood, Barnet. They never said *where* it was. So nobody knows where the road begins. It has no beginning. She thought she was in the Falklands. I can't stand those who carp and criticize. She thought it was an autobahn running into Poland. Tanks will roll to the Dorking Gap and hold back the aliens, the Balkan trash. Frogs. Krauts. That was the end of London. Of her battle with the metropolis, the mob.

To get out you have to go on. There's no other way. To get *in* she had to become another woman, another self. A new person metamorphosed by a change of clothes. The smell of. The crispness of shop-bought cloth. Without previous body print. Red, she thought. For this. For this monstrous box. Red, bought on impulse. On a walk through the City, the first afternoon of spring. Red with white spots. Top and skirt. To see if it worked. Blonde wig. The name, Lucy. Absurd as it was. a tag borrowed from Bram Stoker. As something apposite to the locale, the pervasive aroma of secret recipe meatballs, rolled from the firm flesh of fiord-grazing swine. The panic-scent of vanishing money.

Storage and credit. Erase my credit, erase me. The big metal box devoured credit. A snowstorm of numbers melting from the screen. Potentialities swiped from your life-plan. The box tricked you into embarking on a serpentine journey, a pilgrim path, a ghost trail over flat surfaces. Laminated forest floor, blue plastic stream. Pillars like exclamation marks. The steel-beam rooftree of a fairytale world.

I haven't felt so good, so new, Lucy thought, since the British Museum. The anonymity of that space, those invisible microclimates. The chill of old stone, the neutrality of glass cabinets. My reflection in Dr Dee's mirror. An exchange of passivity. View, don't talk. The reverie of Cycladic figurines and grave goods, recovered shards.

Absorb and escape, unscathed. Primed to buy cards or notebooks or the amber pen with which she is now marking her cat-decorated pad. Her Bastet disguise, her Sekhmet nature.

The scarlet smudge hurt. Kaporal tried to blink away the blood. The play of the eyes tricked him, treated him to unearned frames; a woman in red who might god knows be one of them. *One of them.* Helper, salesperson, facilitator. Floorwalker. A smartly-presented retail whore trained to bring out your unspoken desires. The style had him skewered. A parody of passion. Like a being from a netherworld. a late musical. She had been floated from the gloss of torn paper, brought to life; a glamour model from another era. An awkward lump thickened in his empty pigskin wallet. Fur growing on cured leather, fuzz on suede, hog-bristles on pink. Predator-victim. Lana Turner in a *True Crime* stakeout. Crying from the photoflash. You'd swear, remembering other stars, other confusions of real and performed. Places overwhelmed by a malign topography. *Niagara* . . .

Death will have your eyes. A scalpel-dart of red light, burnt to the arc, flushes him. He follows, stomach gurgling. The obscene cocktail of this red fetch and the kitchens, somewhere beneath them, the vats of pigbrawn and sloppy entrails, hoof and hair. Onions, sage, egg-glue, bread: he gags.

The dough of him, potless Kaporal, rose on a surge. Spear this woman. The drooling sauce smell, ketchup, sizzling meat and her intrusive civet-musk, come-on and keep-away, wreckage of chemical signals, pile-up of conflicting messages. Self-cancelling telegrams. He had to follow.

Have you found the perfect Bed & Bat? Help me. Thirty-five days' vacation is the German national average. She gazes off into the distance, left hand shading eye. He looks east. Not a soul on the beach. No wind. He follows. Arm yourself with the perfect equipment for every job. Help me.

Help was never part of the package. The contract. We think that it's more enjoyable if you're left alone to shop – make decisions. That's true, Kaporal admitted. The advice, the help, made any retail speculation impossible. Couldn't hack it. Kaporal never browsed. He needed the book. The guide he was never going to complete. It was like trying to map water.

She flicked a lick of hair that had flapped over her eye. She winked. He followed.

They met in the restaurant and took seats that favoured the view over the flooded quarry. Lucy thought she could make out her house, the bedroom. She couldn't be sure. They all looked the same. A sinking sun fired distant windows. Their backs to London. Mina, she felt, was rather pale. Her friend needed a holiday. Marriage had frayed her. She toyed with the lunch, left indentations of bright tines in the heap of cooling meat-grains. She sipped her red wine. Moistened the creases in her lips.

Kaporal's torso was on a hook. He was peeled like a kebab, bone and gristle into the industrial mincer. A grinding and spitting, a cough or two. And the human meat was smooth as paste. Rendered. Kaporal rendered, flour-dusted, dipped in gravy.

Bluebeard's Castle in reverse. The bachelor stripped by his bride. He had followed the scarlet woman, false chamber after false chamber, library to bedroom to playpen to kitchen. A hessian screen. A locked door. That delicious meat smell. he couldn't help himself. He drooled, dribbled. His map would be olfactory: pine resin, cardboard, leather.

The locked door. The weariness. She'd vanished. Doorknob carved like a cat's head. The sudden drop in temperature. The hooks, knives, the slate-tables with their draining channels. The smiling butchers. That curious detail, the ball of chalk. With which his outline had been marked on the chart.

Just like a billiard table, Kaporal thought. Falling backwards into the wave, hearing pebbles clatter in the undercurrent. His neck taut, a thick vein pulsing. The eater eaten.

Caught Out

Aydin Mehmet Ali

"They caught him with his lover. His mother and his wife's brother set a trap for him and caught him. He had this extra flat. His wife and he bought it with the money from their wedding. You know what it's like . . . that's what happens at weddings. They collect all that money pinned onto their clothes all the way down to the floor . . . and they bought a flat with it. His wife had a flat already, her grandmother used to live in it and she died or something, I don't quite know, so they had two flats.They bought both of them from the Council.

"I couldn't cope with him. He was so unpredictable, so immature. He was becoming deranged. He rang me a few times and I just gave up after a while I couldn't cope with him. It's not worth it. You have to face what's happening to you and tell your mother at least. Fathers . . . never mind, leave them out of it." and he swipes his hand away as though shooing a fly. The importance of fathers could not be more powerfully dismissed than with that gesture! Shoo . . . out of my life! "But your mother who gave birth to you, who loved you . . . you have to tell her. You can't pretend."

"What about you?" she asks watching him and laughing at his humorous way of dealing with his life. He is a market stall holder. He sells women's clothes in Ridley Market, Hackney. Women come and look at his clothes while he talks to her. As the wind blows he instinctively grabs his giant umbrella handle set up to protect his wares from the rain.

"How much is this?" insists a black woman. "Twenty-five pounds, darling." without turning his face in the middle of his story.

"What size is it?" comes another insistent question.

"Twelve" is the non-committed answer. She is too obviously above that size but does not accept defeat and defies classification by others.

"Haven't you got a size fourteen?"

"I've got a size sixteen!"

She shrinks, "Sixteen!" she says, touching her breast tenderly with her finger-tips, insulted, and smiles shyly to the woman he is talking to who had turned her eyes to look at her in the middle of the story.

"If one buys one thing, they all want the same thing; if one stops to look, they all stop to look!"

"How did they catch them?" she asks.

"I suppose someone must have twigged that something was going on and they set a trap for them. They caught them in bed together, there was no denying it. Then the whole thing started . . . screams, shouts, the whole family became involved, a big scandal! They, the family, reported it to the police, the lover was deported. You should have seen it! It was so messy, a real Arabesque story . . . the Turkish films had nothing on this!" He laughs then his face creases up again as though he bit into something bitter.

"And he was terrible. He just didn't know how to handle it. He freaked out. He did things he shouldn't have done." He straightens out a black suit with embroidery on the collar. He looks at passers-by, would-be customers, with a quick glance.

"He wanted to give his lover the impression he was really well off. He borrowed money from everywhere and everyone! He cheated lots of people, he did really horrible things, he swindled his friends. He was so much in debt. then he went to Cyprus and checked into one of these expensive hotels. If he had put together four or five thousand pounds he blew it all at this hotel. Golden Sands. Trying to impress his lover. He just blew it all!" He makes an expansive open fan gesture with his hand and stops.

"Do you know it?" he asks.

She says no with the slight upward movement of her head and the raising of her eye-brows.

"Anyway, it's this really expensive place in Girne. So they stayed there; he spent all his money on his lover. They ate, drank, went to discos. As you know, Cyprus is expensive, It didn't last long. He spent it all. They were then kicked out of the hotel. He had nowhere to go. No one would have him. So he came back to London. His wife wouldn't have him back, of course. His mother didn't want to know. He'd disgraced the family! Others are after him because he swindled everyone. So he can't ask for help from anyone. There he is . . . you see him here and there, destitute. To tell you the truth, I don't think it was worth it. Not the way he did it anyway."

"What happened to the lover?" she asks.

"Oh, nothing! What can the lover do? In Cyprus; waiting for him to sort things out from this end. The lover obviously wants to come here . . . but not much chance with these immigration laws as they are. And if you haven't got anyone, no one will look after you. This bloke can't even look after himself let alone his lover."

* * *

"Oh! Vay vay vay! What a surprise! Hosgeldiniz! Hosgeldiniz!"

The expansive mother contained in the latest fashion garment admired on the tall top models on the front covers of magazines opens the door and smiles. She is one of the privileged few who worked in the sweat-shops making those garments for the world's elite so she wore them whether they suited her or not just like other Cypriots making other garments in other sweat-shops.

She welcomes her guests. She is happy and although she had said it was a surprise it wasn't at all. She knew they were coming and she was well prepared for them. She leans over and kisses her brother who has just arrived from Cyprus. She has dressed to make a good impression on him and his family. This time he is here only with his son.

She doesn't like to give the impression that all they do is work long hours. She wants him to think there are other important things in their lives, that they know how to enjoy themselves. It wasn't all about killing themselves in the shop or in the factory to show off their car, their expensively but tastelessly decorated house, the large amount of food and excessive amounts of drinks in the cabinet. Her pink painted cheeks flashed in contrast to her straw tinted hair in an attempt to hide the greys appearing amongst the dark browns. Her gold bracelets and chains and rings were ceremoniously put on to complete the picture of success if not of a comfortable life.

She embraces her brother's son, who is barely twenty, she thinks. He has a smooth skin, dark hair and dark soft eyes. His aftershave as she kisses him reminds her he is a man. She checks herself and her womanly desires. She suddenly becomes conscious that her breasts have rubbed against his body. She pulls herself away and looks at his face for signs of awareness. He smiles in the depths of his eyes to his aunt and tells her she's looking younger than the last time he saw her because he is aware of her efforts to preserve her younger self.

"What is it? Is it the water the soil the air of this London that makes women look young and beautiful?" She laughs him off, sure that he is only being polite and he has not sensed anything. She shows him in.

Behind her, her daughter kisses the cheeks of her cousin formally as appropriate between two young people in their twenties lest there is talk even from the most innocent of contacts. People talk. People invent. People want to add excitement to life. People refuse to accept the dullness of life all around.

Wake up get the children ready send them off take them to school go to work enter that sweatshop early in the morning listen to the crap from the boss who keeps telling you to work harder or else you know there are so many people out there ready to jump in go to the shop work your guts out trying to make a living go shopping pick up the kids go home cook for the evening eat sit in front of the TV and fall into bed get up in the morning . . .

. . . and at the weekend go to a wedding and engagement reception a circumcision party sit in rows of tables sometimes not sure whether you are in a wedding engagement circumcision party unless you look in the appropriate direction the same food is served the same music played the same dance danced the same money is hung on the breast of the bride groom fiancé circumcised boy you show off your daughters ensure that their wares goods are exhibited to the world ready for the payment from the highest bidder sometimes trouble strikes these young women now a days get off the rails fall for some penniless nobody because they are good looking what sort of choice is that what sort of life would good looks bring how long would good looks last . . .

. . . people want life to be as dramatic as in the Turkish films . . . ahhh! did you see how that gullible girl believed the words of the boy's wicked mother that he was already engaged to someone else he would never marry her he was in love with his fiancé the daughter of the eminent so-and-so the girl was just a plaything for him passing the time after all . . . didn't she know?

Cemaliye kisses her distant cousin's cheeks with the appropriate degree of propriety. Distant not because of proximity of relationship but they have not met each other often and they don't know each other at all. Cemaliye was born in London, in Islington, when it was a home for Turkish Cypriots in the late sixties. Her father was an auxiliary policeman in Limassol. Soon after the declaration of independence in 1960 he took the hand-out package for services delivered to the Great British Empire and came to London. The package consisted of a British passport for him and his wife who was two months pregnant, two tickets and £1,000 pocket money to start a new life. Compared to what he would have faced it was a good package. He had to escape from the possible reprisals of all those Greek Cypriots he had beaten the shit out of and imprisoned under instructions from the British officers. He was only doing his job, obeying instructions. He sensed that his compatriots – no matter that they are known as gentle island people more in love with life than vendettas – he didn't feel they would welcome him with open arms once the British Empire withdrew in 1960 leaving well stocked well guarded annexes of the Empire in Dheikelia, Episkopi and Akrotiri. The Middle East can still be controlled from the unsinking aircraft carrier, as Cyprus is aptly named. England promised a new life where no one would know who he was and no one would care anyway.

She was born into the family, as the third daughter and her childhood passed in the working men's cafe her parents ran in Islington. She forever remembers the eating and smelling of greasy chips sausages bacon and fried eggs. Greasy chips and egg came out of her pores almost. And bacon was not supposed to have been allowed in the house let alone cooked and served by Muslims. That was one of the first jobs her father had; he moved from one to another until now where he had a grocer's shop in Haringey.

Her cousin was handsome. Slim. He had beautiful eyes and long eyelashes and a very dazzling smile . . . and full lips. He brushed his curly black hair back. But he didn't seem to be aware of his own looks or the effect he had on women around him or maybe he was too used to it. He was so natural with women.

Behind her came her husband who shook hands heartily and welcomed the father and the son whom he had not seen before and now he was related to. They had become his uncle and his cousin as well. He was also a second-generation Cypriot but came when he was one and grew up in Haringey.

He grew up with Afro-Caribbean boys because they were more daring and would get up to more tricks than anyone else. He didn't like the English boys because they didn't like him. They called him "bubble-n-squeak, Greek", even though they knew he wasn't a Greek Cypriot, But it was all the same to them. The black boys stuck together and didn't let anyone mess with them. There were a couple of Turkish Cypriot boys in the gang and they did everything together. Not that they did anything nasty; just the fact that a group of Black boys walked together was enough to worry other people around them. He picked up Jamaican language, one of the best collections of Reggae records, swear words and they picked up Turkish ones. His mother always shouted at him for going around with those "Arabs", her word for Afro-Caribbean people. Why couldn't he stick with his own kind or, even better, with the white boys? But she was polite to the boys when they came to call for Ahmet and even offered them things to eat, things she had made for the family. In her heart of hearts she knew that the boys were all right and were some mother's child like her own. They were nice boys. It was just the neighbours. What would Pembe Hanim say if she saw Ahmet hanging around with these "Arab" boys. What would she say? It would be all over the community, that she, she wasn't able to control her son who was going around with the "Arabs". She would be embarrassed, her reputation would be damaged. What reputation, Ahmet would ask her when she would go on and on; what reputation indeed? It was just that the community would talk, there would be gossip, she didn't want gossip; and then it would also affect the reputation of his little sister. She was only six but as she grew up, if he continued to hang around the "Arab" boys and they were to come around when she was older . . . no! That wouldn't do! That was the limit! Wait till she gets a couple of years older and he would have to stop this nonsense. She wasn't going to have the *kismet* of her daughter cut off because of this nonsense of hanging around the "Arab" boys because he felt more comfortable or safer with them. He had to stop this nonsense.

Then he was married off to Cemaliye. It was as traditional as the marriage of their fathers and mothers except making use of all the latest gadgets, like filming the event. They met at one of those well-known weddings one Sunday afternoon in one of the big banquet halls, the Aksaray – White Palace indeed! And they had their wedding there in the end.

He gave in to pressures to marry from his mother. He tried to resist but in the end he ran out of excuses according to his mother's set of values or good reasons according to his own which he thought might be acceptable. He held out until the age of twenty-five then his father joined in.

They wanted him to stop running around with his friends, disco here night-club there wasting his money wasting his life he needed to settle down a wife would do him good and a couple of kids would settle his madness he was getting old no woman would have him soon he was wasting his life he would be too old to have children and be a proper father what did he want to be a father at 40 he wouldn't even be able to kick a football around in the park with his sons if he left it any later he would be an old man his hair was going to fall out soon and women don't like bald men didn't he know his father did not feel he could support him like this any longer he had to make up his mind was he going to get involved in the business and work hard or what he didn't think Ahmet could take the responsibility like this but if he was to marry then he would feel responsible for his family and would settle down and yes they would concede to him choosing his wife as long as she was the daughter of a good family and her parents had taken good care of her he wasn't going to choose some barefooted beggar was he to leave it to them . . . they would see him right.

Everything was arranged; all he did was to say yes to their suggestion when they pointed her out at a cousin's wedding. It felt like they were out shopping. She seemed OK, lively, was dancing with her friends, she looked at him teasingly across the tables when she realized her family and he were looking at her. She had guessed. The boy she secretly loved was married to a richer girl eight months earlier. She was devastated, thought about committing suicide but in the end went to Cyprus and stayed for five months. She came back knowing she had no choice but to go on. She had to find someone to be married to – maybe the feeling of being married and having children make the heartache go away. She loved children. She wanted to have one as soon as she was married. And in time she might love her husband. That's what the elders kept saying anyway. In time she would love her husband and forget about her love.

Do you think we loved anyone, they would say, we just married them and here we are. What's so different about you lot? Just because you are younger and you have a bit more freedom to say yes or no, more than we did, nothing much has changed for women. It's the same story. In the end you will marry someone, you will serve him, you will cook for him, clean his house, have his kids, put up with his funny ways and just get on. No use moaning or groaning about your lot and thinking you can do something about it. He is your husband, he has to look after you. That's it! Sometimes you younger girls think you can do things differently from us. It's all the same and don't talk about love. What's love? What's that got to do with anything?

They were married six months later. That was a year ago. What was it like? She couldn't complain. He didn't have bad habits. He went to his Mum a lot. He went out with his friends a lot, the ones who came to his wedding. Lots of people his age, some Black friends, they all seemed to have hung around since they were young. They played football together for one of the teams in the Turkish League. Most were married like him only one or two were still unmarried. Her own marriage wasn't exciting. He didn't take her out as much as she wanted. And she was getting bored on her own in the house they bought together. She was working half a day at the dry cleaners but that was almost just to get her out of the house and contribute to the bills. She wasn't enjoying it, she wasn't enjoying married life. She felt more lonely than when she was in her mother's house, at least she had her sisters when she was at home. That's why she would go to her Mum's every minute she had.

And a baby? Well, it wasn't happening. Every time she wanted it he moved away. At first he tried and she didn't know what she was supposed to do. She thought she was doing something wrong, putting him off, he gave her that impression anyway. She would hug him and caress him and he would get excited and come inside her then all of a sudden she would realize that she couldn't feel him. She would try her best and push her body against him, open her legs wider, try to hold him. He would try and they would both struggle because that's what it seemed like. After the struggle he would roll off and leave her bewildered, lying on her back in the dark, because it was always in the dark, not knowing if something had happened, if he had come, if this was all there was to it. She would lie there afraid to do anything, feeling hunger rising from her inner depths, from her cunt, unsatisfied, unfulfilled, screaming with hunger. He would say nothing, turn his back on her. Sometimes he would turn around and hug her, wrap her in his arms and kiss her hair. She felt maybe he loved her then. In time they would learn how to do it and in time they would have children and then everything would be OK. Her mother told her to be patient every time she tried to broach the subject.

She had nothing to worry about he wasn't beating her up was he he wasn't spending his money on whores and other women especially English women was he he went out with his mates every weekend and that was normal men like going with their friends for a drink after being at home all week he was looking after her providing for her wasn't he not all of them are good at it you know they might talk about it a lot show off and put themselves about and walk around thrusting their below the belt area forward to show what a big bundle they had but when they have to do it when it counts they shrivel up don't worry about it she would laugh wiping her tears from the corner of her eyes doubling over and slapping her hands at her own explicitness secretly worrying that her daughter had not been sexually satisfied yet and was living with that frustration who knows what might happen if she continued to be sexually frustrated she can't carry on for ever can she if only she could get pregnant that would take things off her mind she would be occupied God forbid she might want to divorce him or even worse go with another man she would die of the shame of it wasn't it crazy all these years she was like a mad woman making sure that nothing happened to her daughter that nothing happened to her thin membrane her virginity symbol stretched across her vagina's entrance and here she was now that that damn membrane didn't matter she wasn't doing anything and wasn't enjoying anything wasn't life a fuck-up!

Everyone piled into the meticulously kept *misafir odasi*, guest room as it is called in Turkish. No one is allowed to even walk into it during normal family life. it is the preserve of the guests. the family can only use it when guests arrive. The best china is in the glass cupboard, so are the crystal glasses of all shapes for whisky wine water perfectly lined up small ornaments of china glass tall vases figurines dancing playing the violin being hobos dogs on their hind legs an inevitable map of Cyprus made into a clock coffee cups with an ancient map of Cyprus on them colourful plastic flowers in vases dotted about the room brand new looking sparkling furniture reproductions of some heavy palace furniture . . . all tasteless. Finished off with the big glass chandelier maybe even crystal. And the obligatory untouchable drinks cabinet containing collections of whiskies wines miniatures all lined up leering at the guests with the knowledge that they will never be drunk, they are there to be looked at and for him to feel proud of his achievement of his collection. Everything in the room belonged to her, she had chosen it, she had arranged it, but that belonged to him. She wasn't even allowed to clean it.

"What would you like to drink? We have practically everything you might like," she says without giving them a chance to ask but also preparing the ground for him to enter and show off his collection and knowledge. Cemaliye sits next to her husband on the long sofa. The uncle and the son opposite them on the comfortable chairs near each other. Mother is fussing to provide nuts and savoury nibbles while father shows off with his drinks, both giving the performance of the ever attentive generous hosts to their guests. Cemaliye's eyes keep flowing back to her uncle's son. She catches the curve at the side of his lips, the laughter in his eyes, his fingers folded around the glass. She hides her fascination with him quite well; she has had a lifetime of practice. She is careful to address him as little cousin as a term of endearment but also highlighting to everyone that at twenty-two she is three years his senior. He responds with his casual warm smile and reserved manner. He doesn't seem to need to speak in a manner that draws attention to himself or need to impress anyone.

His father tells Cemaliye that marriage seems to have done her good, she's looking good. he then makes the usual sexual innuendo and jokes with Ahmet. He in turn confirms the correctness of the observation with his hearty laughter. yes, indeed, once you give these women a bit of . . . they blossom, thanks to us. Cemaliye shifts her shoulders and smiles as befits a modest married woman. Her eye catches her cousin's smiling eyes which move from Ahmet's laughter to her uneasy smile.

During dinner, Ahmet and her cousin sit next to each other. She watches them loosening up as the evening progresses and is pleased that they are getting on so well. She hadn't seen her husband so friendly towards her side of the family. They are drinking, she thinks, it's also the influence of the drink. By two o'clock in the morning all the men are drunk, the women are tipsy and laughing a lot, humouring the men.

Men are telling stories of their youth and telling the younger ones that they don't know what life is about. Did they live through EOKA, did they live through TAKSIM and VOLKAN? What was that . . . lining fourteen year old schoolboys in the schoolyard and telling them they had to be soldiers and protect the *Yavru Vatan,* baby country, and that *Ana Vatan,* the motherland, had ordered it.

"I shit on it! You pimps! If you thought it was easy why don't you come and do it?" demands Cemaliye's father of long-suppressed ghosts. He swings his hand across his chest pointing to the space between his feet. "Oh! Yeah! Easy, innit? You send your sons to Turkey, pretend they are at college or university so that they are safe, and you tell everyone to send their sons to fight. They are sacrificial lambs but not your sons. If your arse is tight come and fight and let your son fight too!" The uncle talks of the officer from Turkey who came to the village and threatened everyone to turn up for duty the following night. "The village shepherd didn't because no one had told him, he was such a meek person I suppose no one thought of it. They found him dead after a few days by his animals in the valley. The Turkish officer blamed the Greeks for the bloody murder but everyone in the village knew it was the officers from Turkey. What funny names they had; Wind, Storm and such like. Our people weren't such brutes as to do such a cold-blooded thing to someone from their own village, he was only a poor bastard trying to earn his living."

He sniffles trying to suppress tears. Let's drink, he shouts as he staggers across to the whisky bottle – a dash of Coke takes the bitterness away. The music goes on, Turkish, Greek and a bit of English. The gathering dances, the older ones collapse on the sofa. Ahmet is trying to dance with the cousin. Their arms and legs move leisurely and exaggeratedly slowly courtesy of the drinks. They keep reaching out, balancing themselves or helping the other balance as he staggers. At one stage they look like rams horn-locked in a fight with one arm against each other's neck, the other hand holding onto a whisky glass. Once the dance is finished they hug and slap each other on the back, holding each other up laughing with eyes closed, almost passing out in each other's arms. Congratulating each other for still standing. "How beautifully you dance, kid. Is this what they teach you in Cyprus?" Ahmet says holding the cousin's face in his hands close to his face in his drunken stupor.

* * *

"How beautifully you danced that night. I couldn't keep my hands off you. I couldn't keep my eyes off you. I trembled each time I thought of my lips touching yours. I don't know how I kept my lips off you. I don't know how I managed to control myself in front of all of them."

"You do though . . . don't you? You learn to do it as soon as you realize you desire someone. You must not let anyone suspect a thing . . ." The cousin reaches out and touches the hands holding his face.

They are on the mattress on the floor in the middle of the room. The white sheet acting as curtain at the window filters the sunshine coming into the room falling onto the bed. They are kneeling facing each other. They are naked. Ahmet holds Cem's face in his palms as he did that night they met, his heart beating wildly, his body wanting to burst out of the skin holding it in check. He breaths in Cem's smell. He touches his cheeks, eyes, nose, temples, hair, mouth, lightly, with his slightly parted lips taking in his smells. Kissing him gently afraid of the violence of his own passion. His lips move further down to kiss his neck, his shoulders, his chest. He licks his nipples. He takes them between his lips and plays with them with his tongue until he feels them harden and stand up. He moves his hands down Cem's shoulders, then to his waist, to the small of his back, exploring with his fingers the crevice between his buttocks, his other hand caressing his buttocks in circular, gentle movements. He carefully lays Cem on his back trembling, touching him gently, afraid he may break him, his fingers move to caress the smooth warm skin across his abdomen, navel, down the inside of his legs. Ahmet takes Cem between his legs and on his knees leans over and kisses this body he adores, he licks every inch down to his toes. He sinks his face into his curly sweet smelling mound of hairs and sucks Cem's offering of himself. He fills his mouth with love juices as his heart beats in his head. He turns Cem gently over on his side and nearly cries out as he enters him.

* * *

"Well, they had a key, didn't they. The mother had a key because it was her mother's flat. So the mother and his wife's brother found them in bed together. There was no denying it. There it was. Well, you can imagine the scene can't you! Especially from the mother . . . the mother informed on the boy so he was deported. Ahmet now is wandering around desperate, alone, because he cheated everyone, he owes money to so many people. And frankly, no one wants to help him, they've been stung! And he's gone crazy! He is walking around like a madman. You see him in the cafes, gambling what little money he has. He he will make it big one day and he will bring his lover over. I don't know . . . he lives in cloud cuckoo land. As long as he stays away from me I don't mind. I tried to help him but it's no use . . . he is a liability, he has lost it somewhere . . . he should have told his mother right at the beginning. She would have shouted and screamed but she would have accepted it eventually."

"No love. I don't have that in size twelve. It's too small for you. I have this in size sixteen, would you like to see it?"

She whispers an inaudible no, offended that anyone should take her for a size sixteen and walks away.

The Museum of Desire

John Berger

(For S.G.)

The house stands on one side of a square in which there are tall poplars. The house, built just before the French Revolution, is older than the trees. It contains a collection of furniture, paintings, porcelain, armour, which, for over a century, has been open to the public as a museum. Entry is free, there are no tickets, anybody can enter.

The rooms on the ground floor and up the grand staircase, on the first floor, are the same as they were when the famous collector first opened his house to the nation. As you walk through them, something of the preceding eighteenth century settles lightly on your skin like powder. Like eighteenth century talc.

Many of the paintings on display feature young women and shot game, both subjects testifying to the passion of pursuit. Every wall is covered with oil paintings hung close together. The outside walls are thick. No sound from the city outside penetrates.

In a small room on the ground floor, which was previously a stable for horses, and is now full of showcases of armour and muskets, I imagined I heard the sound of a horse blowing through its nostrils. Then I tried to imagine choosing and buying a horse. It must be like owning nothing else. Better than owning a painting. I also imagined stealing one. Perhaps it would have been more complicated, if one kept the horse, than adultery? Commonplace questions to which we'll never know the answer. Meanwhile I wandered from gallery to gallery.

A chandelier in painted porcelain, the candles held aloft by an elephant's trunk, the elephant wearing green, the porcelain made and painted in the royal factory in Sèvres, first bought by Madame Pompadour. Absolute monarchy meant that every creature in the world was a potential servant, and one of the most persistent services demanded was Decoration.

At the other end of the same gallery was a bedroom commode which belonged to Louis XV. The inlay is in rosewood, the rococo decorations in polished bronze. Unthinkingly I laid my notebook on it. The gallery attendant politely picked it up and handed it back to me, shaking his head.

Most of the visitors, like me, were foreigners, more elderly than young, and all of them slightly on tiptoe, hoping to find something indiscreet. Such museums turn everyone into inquisitive gossips with long noses. If we dared, and could, we'd look into every drawer.

In the Dutch part of the collection, we passed drunken peasants, a woman reading a letter, a birthday party, a brothel scene, a Rembrandt, and a canvas by one of his pupils. The latter intrigued me immediately. I moved on and then quickly came back to look at it several times.

This pupil of Rembrandt was called Wilhem Drost. He was probably born in Leyden. In the Louvre in Paris there is a Bathsheba painted by him which echoes Rembrandt's painting of the same subject painted in the same year. Little else today is known about him.

The canvas, that intrigued me, showed a woman, three-quarter face, looking slightly to her right, towards the spectator. She was about thirty years old, she wore a hair clip decorated with tiny pearls in her swept-up hair, and a *décolleté* and dark dress, which her right hand was touching lightly under her right breast.

I decided to do a drawing of her in my notebook. A poor drawing, even if it caught a little of her expression. It allowed me, however, to take something tangible away with me. There were no photographs available, and I did not want her expression, her posture, above all her message, to be lost in some vague generalization. Perhaps she had never been more herself than at the moment when she sat for and inspired this portrait. The poor drawing is here on the table now as I write.

The painted portrait plays a trick, one of the oldest in the world. (Bathsheba was obliged to play it: the trick of appearing to address a stranger, whilst thinking of somebody else.) For an instant the spectator may suppose that the gestures and smile of the woman in Amsterdam are addressed to him. Yet obviously this is not the case.

She was not looking at any spectator. She was looking hard at a man she desired, imagining him as her lover. And this man could only have been Drost. The only thing we know for certain about Drost is that he was desired precisely by this woman.

I made the drawing, not only because I was thinking of Drost's story, but also because I was reminded of something of which one is not usually reminded in museums. To be so desired – if the desire is also reciprocal – renders the one who is desired fearless. No suit of armour from the galleries downstairs ever offered, when worn, a comparable sense of protection. To be desired is perhaps the closest anybody can reach in this life to feeling immortal.

Whilst I was thinking something like this, I heard her voice. Not a voice from Amsterdam, a voice from the great staircase in the house. It was high-pitched yet melodious, precise yet rippling, as if about to dissolve into laughter. Laughter shone on it like light through a window onto satin. Most surprising of all, it was resolutely a voice speaking to a crowd of people; when it paused there was silence. I couldn't distinguish the words, so my curiosity forced me, without a moment's hesitation, to return to the staircase. Twenty or more people were slowly coming up it. Yet I couldn't make out who had been speaking. All of them were waiting for her to begin again.

"At the top of the staircase on the left you will see a three-tiered embroidery table, a woman's table, where she left her scissors and her needlework and her work could still be seen, which was better don't you think than hiding it away in a drawer? Locked drawers were for letters. This piece belonged to the Empress Josephine. The little oval blue plaques, which wink at you, are by Wedgwood."

I saw her for the first time. She was coming up the staircase alone. Everything she wore was black. Flat black shoes, black stockings, black skirt, black cardigan, a black band in her hair. She was the size of a large marionette, about four feet tall. Her pale hands hovered or flew through the air as she talked. She was elderly and I had the impression that her thinness was to do with slipping through time. Yet there was nothing skeletal about her. If she was like one of the departed, she was like a nymph. Around her neck she wore a black ribbon with a card attached to it. On the card was printed the famous name of The Collection and, in smaller letters, her own name. Her first name was Amanda. She was so small that the card looked absurdly large, like a label pinned to a dress in a shop window, announcing a last-minute bargain.

"In the showcase over there you can see a snuff box made of carnelian and gold. In those days young women as well as men took snuff. It cleared the head and sharpened the senses." She raised her chin, threw her head back and sniffed.

It is hard to describe her face. I studied it again and again and each time, it shifted like a page being turned in a book.

"This particular snuff box has a secret drawer in which the owner kept a tiny gouache portrait, no larger than a postage stamp, of his mistress. Look at her smile. I would say it was she who gave him the snuff box. Carnelian is a red variety of agate, mined in Sicily. The colour perhaps reminded her in some way of him. Most women, you see, see men as either red or blue." She shrugged her frail shoulders. "The red ones are easier."

When she stopped talking, she did not look at the public but turned her back and walked on. Despite her smallness, she walked much faster than her followers. She was wearing a ring on her left thumb. I suspect that her black hair was a wig, for I'm sure she preferred wigs to rinses.

Our walk through the galleries began to resemble a walk through a wood. This was a question of how she placed us, herself and what she was talking about. She consistently prevented us from crowding around whatever she was explaining. She pointed out an item as if it were a deer to be glimpsed as it crossed our path between two distant trees. And wherever she directed our attention, she always kept herself elusively to the side, as if she had just stepped out from behind a tree. I had the impression that we turned in circles and that we passed the same spot two or three times. Once we passed a rainbow and once we came upon a statue under the trees, its marble turning a little green because of the shade and dampness.

"The statue depicts Friendship consoling Love," she murmured, "for Madame de Pompadour's relation with Louis XV is now platonic, which hasn't stopped her wearing – has it? – the most gorgeous dress."

One gilded time-piece after another chimed two downstairs: the beginning of the afternoon.

"Now we go," she said, holding her head high, "to another part of the wood, the painter has made it morning here, so all is fresh, and everyone is freshly dressed – including the young lady on the swing. No statues of Friendship, all the statues here are Cupids. The Swing was put up in the Spring. One of her slippers – you notice? – has already been kicked off! Intentionally? Unintentionally? Who can tell? As soon as a young lady, freshly dressed, sits herself there on the seat of the swing, such questions are hard to answer, no feet on the ground. The husband is pushing her from behind. Swing high, swing low. The lover is hidden in the bushes in front of her where she told him to be. Her dress – it's less elaborate, more casual, than Madame de Pompadour's and frankly I prefer it – is of satin with lace flounces. Do you know what they called the red of her dress, they called it peach, though personally I never saw a peach of that colour, any more than I ever saw a peach blushing. The stockings are white cotton, a little roughish compared too the skin of the knees they cover. The garters, pink ones to match the slippers, are too small to go higher up the leg without pinching. Notice her hidden lover. The foot, which lost the slipper, is holding up the skirt and petticoats high – their lace and satin rustle softly in the slipstream – and nobody, I promise you, nobody in those days wore underwear! His eyes are popping out of his head. As she intended him to do, he can see all."

Abruptly the words stopped, and she made a rustling noise with her tongue behind clenched teeth, as though she were pronouncing only the consonants of the words *lace* and *satin* without the vowels. Her eyes were closed. When she opened them, she said: "Lace is a kind of white writing which you can only read when there's skin behind it."

The guided tour was soon over, and before anybody could ask a question or thank her, she disappeared into an office behind the book counter.

When she came out, half an hour later, she had taken off the ribbon around her neck with its card, and put on a black overcoat. If she had stood beside me, she would have come up to my elbows, no more. In her face I could find nothing. It was blank, peacefully blank.

She walked briskly down the front steps of the house into the square where the poplars are. She was carrying an old flimsy Marks and Spencer's plastic bag which looked as if it might tear, because whatever was in it was too heavy.

In the bag were a cauliflower, a pair of resoled shoes and nine wrapped presents. The presents were all for the same person and each one was numbered and tied up with the same golden twine. In the first was a sea shell. A small conch about the size of a child's fist, perhaps the size of her fist. I was never close enough to really measure. The shell was the colour of silverish felt, veering towards peach. If one turned it to look inside, the peach was more vivid. The swirls of its brittle encrustations resembled the lace flounces on the dress of the woman on the swing, and its polished interior was as pale as skin habitually sheltered from the sun.

The second present was a bar of soap, bought at a Boots Chemist shop and labeled Arcadia. It smelt of a back you can touch but can't see because you're facing the front.

The third packet contained a candle which, when lit, smelt of black coffee. The price tag said .85 EURO. In the fourth was another candle. Not made of wax this time but in a glass tumbler which looked as if it were full of sea water with sand and very small shells at the bottom. The wick appeared to be floating on the surface. A printed label stuck on to the glass said: Never leave a burning candle unattended.

The fifth present was a paper bag of a brand of sweets called wine gums. This brand has existed for a century. Probably they are the cheapest sweets in the world. Despite their very varied and acid colours, they all taste of pear drops. For me (but they were not for me) no other taste I know evokes so sharply my early childhood. Their flavour remains the flavour of pleasure itself, before I could tie my own shoe laces in double bows.

Her next present was a metal lantern in which one would put a candle before hanging it by a window or going out to open a gate. The colour of its glass was a transparent but dark purplish blue. The colour of certain notes played on a saxophone: the colour of unlit methylated spirits at night.

The seventh was a radio cassette of Saint Augustine nuns singing *O Filii et Filliae*, a thirteenth century plainsong written by Jean Tisserand. Her eighth was a box of graphite sticks and pencils. Soft. Medium. Hard. Traces made by the Soft graphite are jet black like thick hair, and traces made by the Hard are like hair turning grey. Graphite, as skins do, has its own oils. It is a very different substance from the burnt ash of charcoal. Its sheen when applied on paper is like the sheen on lips. With one of the graphite pencils she had written on a piece of paper which she put in the box: "On the last hour of the last day, one must remember this."

Her ninth present was a kind of embroidered pin cushion, very small, in the form of a heart. Its stuffing smelt of cinnamon and a perfume I do not know. A note, written in her handwriting, was wrapped around it. It read: "When a man is loved he leaves the chorus like long ago and becomes a king."

The Train Game

Efe Okogu

I lost my virginity to Juliette Sorrenson by the side of the tracks moments after the 6:26 to Cockfosters almost crushed me to death. Afterwards we watched the sun rise on a new day; a new year. It was January the first, 2000, my fifteenth birthday, the end of a millennium; the end of my childhood. A week later, we stood on a rooftop watching the sunset, her knife in her left hand, her clothes drenched in her stepfather's blood.

That New Year's Eve was my first spent without my mother. It was meant to be the greatest night of my life: counting down in Trafalgar Square with my mates and getting off with some random girl. It was meant to be the night I entered the world of getting pissed and getting laid so I'd be the one bragging for once instead of always listening, envious, to Ahmed or Johno.

It had started out great. Veronica had been flirting with me all night, and for the first time I was hanging out with my mates late at night. My mother is strict so my nights out were few and far between. It had taken weeks of arguing for her to let me out for this. Then just before the countdown, I saw Ahmed making out with Veronica. She'd been after him so had talked to me all night to make him jealous. Now it was my turn.

Midnight struck; I watched the fireworks explode in a riot of colour, the sparks raining down on the heads of the gathered masses like fairy dust from the gods, as if to say for this one brief moment everything was going to be OK. For a moment, I believed. Then I turned round to find myself alone. In the far corner of the square, I saw Ahmed, Veronica and the others run up the stairs towards Piccadilly Circus.

I yelled after them and Veronica turned, looked me dead in the eyes and kept moving. They ditched me.

A beautiful redhead ran by laughing, her long curly hair stroking my face. I grabbed her by the shoulders and kissed her. She smiled good-naturedly then kicked me in the balls. My screams blended perfectly into the laughter of the night.

I bought some alcohol and walked along the Thames. My memories of the rest of the night are sketchy. Time flowed from me like the river, filled with unfulfilled wishes like deformed fishes, mutated by the filth of the city.

The next coherent memory I have is of sitting on the gravestone of Richard O'Connor, BELOVED HUSBAND AND FATHER – TAKEN FROM US BEFORE HIS TIME, smoking a spliff. I was in that surprising moment of clarity between being shitfaced and hungover having an epiphany: I didn't have a single true friend in the world. I wasn't a loner – that would have been cool in a Johnny Depp sort of way – I was a loser.

The Blessed May cemetery at the end of my road sits on a little hill right next to the train tracks. From my vantage point on Richard's grave, who I was beginning to feel very close to, I could look out over the city. Bathed in predawn light and mist, the twinkling lights of the revellers below reminded me of the first time I flew in a plane and saw us approaching a vast black grid lit up by a thousand pinpricks of light. I felt that same excitement now. I wanted to fly. I wanted to die.

A train thundered by, disturbing my reverie, causing the tracks on the other side of the flattened fence that marked the boundary of the cemetery to squeal like a dying cat. Once it was gone, I stepped onto the tracks. It was time for the train game.

I started playing the train game three years ago, right after my father died of cancer. Towards the end, he was as unrecognizable to me as I was to him. The chemo hadn't worked, simply gutted him like a fish of all he was, of who he was. I didn't mind the baldness or the sallowness of his skin so much. It was the way he smiled, as if afraid if he didn't, he'd cry. "Never let them see you cry, son", he'd told me often. Before the cancer, my father almost never smiled. Afterwards, his face became a snapshot of a grin, frozen for eternity, a prison behind which he awaited death. Everyone said it was amazing how well he was handling it but I knew better. So did my mother. That's why she stopped drinking and became the authoritarian I know today. His dying forced her to grow up and I don't think she ever forgave him, but as he's not here, she takes it out on me.

The twin amber lights of an approaching train brought me back to the present; I could tell by its speed that it was a freight, one moment distant, the next mere inches from my face. The familiar fear resurfaced; butterfly kisses from a long-lost loved one trapped in the pit of my stomach, excited at the thought of escape.

The train game is simple. You stand on the tracks watching for a train and once you see it coming you say to yourself, "Give me one good reason why I should step off". Staring into the inevitable face of the alternative puts your insignificant problems into perspective pretty damn quick. Usually. This dawn, however, the squealing cat had become a roaring lion about to bite my head off and I still couldn't think of a thing.

To this day, I don't know whether I would have stepped off anyway, of my own volition, if Juliette hadn't called my name. Let me explain. I'm a coward and have always been. Ever since I realized I wouldn't grow above five foot five and would always be skinny no matter how much I ate. The first time I played the train game, the night of my dad's funeral, I hadn't been able to think of a reason either. My heart was silent so my head intervened and said, "mum." It was a lie and I knew it, but it still saved my pathetic life.

On this morning, I turned and looked left and there she was, her pale face luminescent in the darkness of the graveyard, such that it appeared to float in midair. I jumped. Less than a second later, several hundred tons of rusted metal rolled over the spot where I had been standing.

"Are you crazy? You could have been killed," I imagined she would say.

"Sorry," she said instead. She straddled me and brought her face close to mine. "I couldn't watch you do it." Her brown eyes appeared black, a wall hiding all manner of portents I could not decipher. She kissed me and I was instantly hard. I ran my right hand over her buzzcut hair and reached under her top with my left.

"Fancy a shag," she said. It was not a question. Her slender fingers roughly pulled down my pants and reached down inside. They were cold against the heat she found there. I was throbbing, scared I would come in her hands, so I pulled her fingers away and lifted her up. She slid down on me; I was an orphan coming home. She moaned, pushing me savagely to the ground, pinning my wrists above my head. As she rode me, I stared up into the tree above us and saw a blue plastic bag caught in its dead branches, swaying in the wind, matching our rhythm, and as I exploded within her, she howled, the bag broke free, soared high in the sky, taking all that was blue in my world with it.

We lay there a moment more until I realized I had just lost my virginity six feet above my father's rotting corpse. When I told Juliette she said, "I'm sure he'd have been proud of your performance. I know I am." She was probably right; my father had a weird sense of humour and would have seen the funny side. I once caught him with Linda, my babysitter. I was ten or eleven at the time (this was before the Big C gave him a little C, making it impossible for him to take a piss on his own, let alone get an erection).

He'd looked at me through Linda's ankles and said in his Irish brogue, "When I'm done, son, you want to have a go?" Less than two weeks before, I had confessed to him that I had wet dreams about Linda. Now I wanted to kill him.

"I'm telling mum", I said softly.

"If you do, she'll never let Linda come over again." Linda looked at me wordlessly. I was trapped. Even back then I knew that if I didn't tell my mother, Linda would never respect me, but if I did, I'd never see her again. I was weak but, worse than that, all three of us knew it.

"I hope your cock falls off and you die horribly." If only I'd known about foreshadowing. I didn't shout like a little kid but I did run out so they wouldn't hear me cry. I listened to them laugh and, soon after, grunt in time to the beat of the banging floorboards.

I didn't tell my mother but I think she knew anyway. Mrs Tabitha O'Connor always seemed to know what was going on with everyone. She'd known my father was seriously ill long before the doctors spoke those two words feared by men the world over – "testicular cancer". She was the first source of information on the lives, loves and lies of our North London community. I imagined her as a black widow, sitting at the centre of a vast web of gossip that stretched from Dalston to Seven Sisters. And, as the black widow of a white man, with all that that entailed, she was as much gossiped about as she was gossiped to. And she knew when I walked in the door after escorting Juliette home that morning that something was different.

"Happy birthday," she smiled. "Were you warm enough?"

"Don't worry, I kept warm," I answered.

"Have a good time with your friends?"

"No . . . but I had a good time." She arched her eyebrow and looked at me long and hard.

"Who is she?" she asked.

"You don't know her," I hesitated. "Besides, I don't really

know if we're together. It was a weird night. Anyway, how was your night with Raj?" I asked her, playfully changing the subject. Her eyes turned cold. I'd gone too far.

"Get some sleep," she said and went back to her room. I slapped my forehead with the heel of my palm, feeling like an idiot. Raj was a nice guy, for a lawyer, and I hoped they would get together but that would never happen if she thought there was any hint of impropriety. She still felt it would be a betrayal of my father.

My parents met in the early eighties when my father moved to London from Belfast to seek a better life. There had been trouble back home with the law; I think it had to do with the IRA but I'm not sure. He never spoke of his past and I've never met his side of the family. She was British born and bred, her parents having come over from Jamaica after the end of World War II. He was a janitor at Homerton hospital and she was a nurse. They both worked the graveyard shift and would fuck at every opportunity, even in the mortuary or the X-ray room where they could look into each other's bones and thus need never lie.

With them, sex came first and love later, through acquired intimacy. They were a fun-loving couple. Throughout my childhood, they were always out drinking, partying and getting into all sorts of trouble, be it with rallies or racehorses. They hadn't planned on having me, and my mother was ready to abort, but my father, in a rare Catholic streak, swore he'd leave her if she did, so eight months later they got married and I was allowed into the world. My arrival didn't really slow them down much; an endless string of babysitters took care of my needs as well as my father's.

I fell asleep with a smile on my face, the smell of the graveyard and the smell of sex intermingled in my thoughts.

Juliette new to Hackney Free and Parochial. Like everyone else, I'd noticed her – it was hard not to – but in the past term, I hadn't exchanged a dozen words with her. She was a loner, not beautiful, but by no stretch of the imagination plain or even average-looking. Our French teacher, Madame Coulthard, called her *jolie-laide* with wonder in her voice. Everyone said Juliette was crazy and meant to be on pills. She talked to herself and had a curious way of arching her wrists and flexing her fingers that made me shiver. I'm not sure how tall she was but when we hugged, my head against her bosom, our bodies moulded to each other, the top of my head and the base of her chin in perfect alignment as if we really were made for each other.

Her height was the first thing people noticed about her. Her legs seemed to go on forever. The second thing that struck most people was her hair, hacked short in a crude buzz cut. She wore glasses and, all in all, looked odd.

"Fuck me slowly with a chainsaw." It was her favourite line from her favourite movie. She'd crept up behind me on our first day back at school and was now nibbling on my ear, her arms encircling my small frame. The look on Johno's face was priceless. Was I being shallow because I knew that every other guy in school wanted to get in her pants? Simply put, yes. I wallowed in it as the news spread around the school. It was the beginning.

"Why are you with me?" I asked her that night as we lay on my couch. My mother didn't get home from work till one in the morning, so we had hours to koch in peace. I had just dropped acid for the first time and was watching my emotions creep up the walls like varicose veins. They were beautiful, all but one, and the doubt infiltrated my thoughts like a sharp sword threatening to cut off my balls.

"It's like, I see myself in your eyes. You know? It's clear. Not distorted like with everyone else," she replied.

I nodded. "But when did you . . . ?"

"Know it was you?"

"Yes."

"At the cemetery. But long before that morning."

"How come I never saw you there?"

"I saw you. I watched you for months." In reply to my questioning, somewhat alarmed gaze, she added, "I was attracted to your pain." Her eyes seemed blacker than ever. They became two large glassy stones, heavy with mystery. I didn't understand her, I realized. She was a cypher and I wanted to rhyme her into reason. I fell but forgot to hit the ground, her gaze holding me suspended in space, so I buried my face in her lap and held on for dear life. I pulled down her pink cotton panties and lost myself in the smell. I licked back and forth then gently tugged on her clit with my teeth. I used my little finger to explore her and open her up whilst alternating the rhythm of my tongue. First slow, then fast, then slow again. Her nails traced blood on my back and her legs encircled my head, holding me in place until I was done, until she was done.

"Molly Bloom," she whispered. There were tears in her eyes.

"Tears of joy?" I joked.

"No, you reminded me of something I don't want to forget".

"What?"

"It was a long time ago." She scissored her legs away and stood up.

"Hey, listen, you can tell me anything." I watched her pace back and forth.

"It was a long time ago," she repeated. "It's . . . it's in the past."

"What is?"

"You know I wasn't a virgin when we . . . "

"Sure."

"Well, I've only ever been with one other man but it doesn't count."

"Listen, just because I've never . . . doesn't mean that I expected . . . I mean, I don't care if I wasn't the first."

"But I care. I want you to know that you were the first guy I wanted to do it with."

"So you fucked some jerk and now regret it. Look, we all do stupid things but it's OK. All that matters now is that we're . . . "

"No, wait," she interrupted. "Just listen. This is hard for me but I've got to tell you, otherwise . . . otherwise . . . I don't know, but we'll be just as bad as . . . I mean, I'll be just as . . ." Her tears now flowed free, tinted blue by the flickering light of the muted television.

"Hey, please don't cry." I reached up and held her, her height no impediment to my manhood, as she helpfully lowered her head to rest on my shoulder. After a few seconds she stopped suddenly, pushed me roughly away, wiped her eyes with the back of her left hand and sat down across from me, legs open like a man.

"When I was twelve, I was raped." I moved to stand but she held up a hand, holding me in place. "There's more. It was my stepdad. It only happened the one time; the night they got married. My mom was in the next room. After he was done, he went down on me and said he knew I wanted him because he was able to make me come."

I winced. "Your mum?"

"I told her the next day. He denied it and said I was just trying to cause trouble and break them up. My mum kept saying she had been asleep and didn't know who to believe. She said it was unfair of us to put her in the middle like that. He threw a tantrum and said if she didn't love him enough to know he'd never do such a thing then he didn't want to be with her. She then told me I must have had a nightmare because I was scared of him replacing me. And I was taking those pills at the time so . . . "

"What pills?"

"The doctors give me these pills to take because of my mood swings. They say I'm manic-depressive and bipolar.

That was after my dad left my mom when I was about ten, and I swallowed a bottle of sleeping pills. Anyway, with all that, they just said I was crazy and my mom and stepdad stayed together."

"I don't know what to say. I'm sorry." She shrugged off my platitudes impatiently.

"Like I said, it was a long time ago, but I wanted you to know before you met him."

"If I ever see him, I'll kill him." I stood up and slammed my fist into the wall, taking pleasure in the pain. "Fuck! He can't just get away with it."

"He did." There was no self-pity. "One day, I'll fuck him slowly with a chainsaw. But right now, I need to know you can deal with it." I wasn't sure what she meant. Deal with it how? But I wanted to be her man. She looked so strong, it scared me. I wanted her to be weaker so I could protect her, comfort her. I went over to her and knelt between her legs. I held her thighs and looked up at her.

"I won't even begin to pretend I can understand what you've been through but I'm here for you." Those were the words in my head. But somewhere along the journey to my mouth they disintegrated and all that came emerged was a sob. She comforted me as I cried my blue tears, a deep flood washing my blood clean, blanketing my dreamscapes, stripping my dark flesh from my bones till I was nothing but bone – white; till I was nothing but bone – dry. I fell asleep wrapped in Juliette's suffering, knowing I was warm and safe there, if nowhere else.

I normally didn't go over to Juliette's to pick her up (we'd usually meet at KFC – Kandahar Fried Chicken, and share a bucket), but that Friday her stepdad was away all weekend and wouldn't be back till Monday night. I walked in to find Juliette and her mother arguing and when Juliette's mother saw me, she told me to get out, that there was no way Juliette was going out that night. Before I knew what was happening, Juliette leapt forwards, pulled out a knife from her boot and held it to her mother's throat. I was rooted to the spot, forced into shadow as mother and daughter did what they had to do. A blind man could see that this had been coming for a long time.

Juliette sighed and stroked her mother's long luxurious hair. She hadn't cut it since she was a little girl and it fell to below her waist. It truly was beautiful. The problem was the rest of her: her face looked like the open wound that was the Oklahoma Federal building after Timothy McVeigh had his way. She had the skin of a lizard and something of the same dull expression and green complexion; and to call her fat would be an insult to obesity. I couldn't understand how she had landed Juliette's stepfather until I saw *Lolita* on TV. After that a lot of things began to make sense. At least to me. For some reason, Juliette needed to believe they really had fallen in love.

"I heard you brushing your hair that night," Juliette whispered. There was no need to explain what night she meant. "You were wide awake." Her mother remained silent. "Say something," Juliette said, her anger rising dangerously. A droplet of blood appeared on her mother's neck as if by magic.

"He's my husband. I love him." Juliette stopped stroking her mother's hair and grabbed a handful, tugging hard, smiling when her mother cried out in pain.

"More than you love me. Sometimes I even think you love your hair more than me." Juliette slowly pulled her knife away as if that was the end of the matter, then suddenly brought it back down sharply. I gasped and looked away, not wanting to see. I turned back and sighed with relief as Juliette threw her mother's hair high into the air above them, the strands falling down around the two of them like memories of bad times.

“Let’s get shitfaced”, she said to me.

We hit the clubs, taking LSD religiously, attempting to save our souls through the act of communion perverted – made beautiful; square slices of heaven washed down with the blood of Christ. Time slowed down, stretched out and went AWOL, shattering the illusion of order; chaos was implicit rather than explicit. I felt like we stood still all night but our shadows danced to the strobe lights, connecting on the most basic of one-dimensional levels.

We were rocking it on the floor when some’brer danced up between us. He turned his back to me and raised his arms in the air around Juliette. She stopped moving and slid around him to face me, rolling her eyes for my benefit. He came between us again so I plucked up my courage and said, “Listen, blood, she’s my girl.”

He looked down at me, laughed pointedly, covered my face with his palm, pushed me to the floor and turned back to Juliette. As I struggled to get up, I heard the sound of breaking glass and a scream. The brother lay on the floor, the right side of his face covered in blood, and standing over him was Juliette, the broken end of her blueberry Bacardi Breezer in her left hand. It struck me that the guy could see up my girl’s dress so I ran over and pulled her back. When I touched her, she spun round and almost stabbed me with her anger, coming close to plunging the broken bottle into my eyes.

“I would have killed him,” she said on the night bus home. I tried to ignore her (but that was impossible), angry that she had fought my battle for me. Angrier because I knew I couldn’t have fought it myself.

“No, you wouldn’t,” I said. “You don’t have it in you.”

“Yes I do”, she said, and we both knew she spoke the truth.

She had her head in my lap and now reached into her boot for her knife. “I want you to have this,” she said. “I won’t be needing it any more”. I took it absentmindedly.

Something had been bothering me for a while so now I asked her, “You know those pills you told me about?”

“The sleeping pills I took?”

“No, the other pills. The ones the doctors gave you.”

“Yes?”

“Do you still take them?”

“No.”

“Don’t you need them?”

She closed her eyes and was quiet for a moment. Then she said, “They lie. They’re like quicksand. They give you false hope, false stability”. She opened her eyes and looked straight into mine. “You’re the real deal. As long as I’m with you, I’ll never think of suicide”. I couldn’t meet her eyes so I looked out the window. Ugly patches of frost covered everything, like God’s dandruff, or poisoned icing on a half-eaten cake.

That weekend, we lived off the fumes of sex, drugs and broken beats. In that netherworld of clarity, where moments of purity can last for hours, until the DJ plays the slow song and the lights come on, I realized I had fallen in love. And as we emerged from our sweaty underground nirvana, the world awakened with me, as if from a deep sleep, limbs unfurling, eyes opening to behold the beauty of our rundown metropolis. Dredheads in suits, palefaces in rags, grannies in steel boots, kids with dogtags: this city of the Technicolor people, speaking in a thousand different tongues, all with the same cockney accent, nameless to me, was no longer faceless to me. Through the cracked mirrors of Juliette’s eyes, I came to see my humanity reflected in the glass. For the first time in my life, I was truly happy. It didn’t last.

“I’ve got something important to tell you.” We were sitting on a bench in Stoke Newington Park, throwing stones into the lake and at the pigeons. Juliette stared, expressionless into the horizon, as if the answer to all her unvoiced questions lay on the other side.

"Oh God. You're pregnant," I said

"No, worse. You know my stepdad is in Turkey right now?" I nodded. "Well, he called last night to say he got the promotion he's been after. He's being transferred to Istanbul. We're moving in June, as soon as school lets out." We sat side by side barely touching. There was nothing to say. As a fifteen-year-old kid, hard as it is to accept, there are some things that are just beyond your control.

That night, I got some more life-changing news. Raj had proposed to my mother and she'd said yes. She was now going to be Mrs Tabitha Awad. The engagement party was that Monday night at the Hindu community centre in Dalston. It was an old school auditorium converted for occasions like this. I should have been happy for her – I *was* happy for her – but all I could think about was Juliette, sunbathing while some Turkish hunk rubbed suntan lotion on her bare back. And it wasn't paranoia. Once she left, I had no idea if I'd ever see her again and I couldn't expect her to be faithful to a memory. I would never ask. I was drowning in teenage bullshit angst, magnified, because for once, it was justified.

At the party, Juliette and I were sitting in one of the old classrooms in a circle with some mates and the school janitor, koching, smoking a spliff, when her stepfather walked in. My mother, in the spirit of family, had invited him without my knowledge. It was the first time I met him face to face. And the last.

"Hi, honey", he smiled at Juliette. "Can we talk?" He looked around and added, "Hello, everyone." Juliette looked at me pleadingly, a cornered animal. Her stepfather spotted me. "So you're my little girl's boyfriend. She's told me all about you."

I stood up, ignoring his extended hand, saying, "And she's told me all about you." He reached forward and gripped my hand, effortlessly crushing my bones. I tried to pull away but he held on, looking me dead in the eyes, a little smile on his face. Without turning round, he said to Juliette, “Come on, sweetheart, we need to talk. It’s about your mother.”

As Juliette reluctantly stood up, I said, “I’ll come with you.”

“No!” he said sharply, then added in a softer tone, “Family only.” I was about to say something more when I realized everyone was watching us, so I kept quiet and watched them walk out. As they left, I realized this was the first time they’d seen each other since Juliette gave her mother her much-needed haircut. As tall as Juliette was, he dwarfed her, his massive paw encircling her small waist.

A month later, I climbed into Juliette’s window and found her wrists slit. She’d called me, after a month without contact, to see this: her life (and thus her pain) being pumped out of her veins by her broken heart.

It worked. I bound her wrists with improvised strips of my Batman T-shirt and sat down to write this story. But first I wrote this poem, my first and last:

> After piecing together the fractal fragments
> of her shattered life
> like so many serrated shards of sunlight,
> the jagged edges sliced through her wrists
> like lust through reason,
> forcing her world into shadow,
> till my entire world was nothing,
> but the twin scarlet pools
> coalescing around her broken form.

Some rich feminist lawyer took Juliette on as a Legal Aid case, and even raised bail money. Normally, murder suspects are kept on remand but with Juliette being a girl and so young, the case had serious high profile. No judge would have dared keep her locked up.

The trial had just begun and the story was all over the news. Even though Juliette's mother testified that the rape had taken place, and a psychiatrist testified that all the trauma Juliette had been through, as well as the imminent move to Turkey, combined with her not taking her medication, had driven her over the edge, it was obvious she was going to be found guilty of killing her stepfather. She'd been found sitting next to his body, covered in his blood, holding her knife, the murder weapon, yet she refused to speak about what had happened, and also refused to plead temporary insanity.

But you know all this. What you don't know is that she's innocent. You have the wrong person. I killed her stepfather. I followed them from the classroom onto the rooftop. I saw red; the sky drenched in scarlet hues. I hid behind a chimney-stack, the ethereal wisps masking me from view, souls of the soon-to-be departed. He was yelling in her face, telling her that in this world, you couldn't just do what you wanted to and not pay the price. He was talking about Juliette's mother's hair but I marvelled that he couldn't see the irony of his words. He was playing the concerned husband, which angered me, but that's not why I killed him.

It was when he softened his voice, stroked her face, said he was worried about her, just wanted what was best for her. On the surface, this was perfectly normal behaviour but the elephant he was ignoring was just too big. He'd raped her and was now playing the concerned dad? She was obviously used to it because she was nodding her head, but it offended me. It offended me greatly. His back was turned to me so I crept up behind him and pulled out the knife Juliette had given me. I then jumped on his back and slit his throat. At the last moment, Juliette cried out, "No!" But it was too late. His blood fountained into the air, briefly staining the rising moon, then blending perfectly into the setting sun (as if both had been painted by the same master's brush), before splattering all over Juliette.

I called her to run with me as I fled, but she just stood there. I couldn't understand her. For once I was strong – I had just solved all our problems with one clean slice – yet all she could do was weep for the bastard. In an instant I saw that, despite everything, he was the only father she knew and she loved him. I had always wondered how she could abide the man's presence on the planet, let alone in her home. Now I began to understand how she could watch him eat cornflakes, drink beer, watch TV, pick his nose, smile, laugh, fart, breathe, without the memory of the night he took her by force driving her to commit mass murder. In my confusion, I dropped the knife and she picked it up, masking my prints with hers. I ran, afraid she might come after me.

Well, now you know. By the time you read this confession, I'll be dead. You can find my body on the tracks next to the Blessed May cemetery. Please tell Juliette I love her and never meant to fuck her slowly with a chainsaw. It just sort of happened. Tell her I'm sorry that I was too small to be her man. Tell her, this time, I'm playing the train game for real.

John Fortune

A. Sivanandan

Lindiwe was sure she was being followed. By the same man. Not stalked, but followed. Nobody stalked anybody in King's Cross. Or followed anybody, for that matter, except to cadge the price of a drink. Lindiwe was used to that. She had been working at the Centre on Poverty on Caledonian Road for about five years now, and in that time she had seen that part of King's Cross, east of the station, decline from a busy, albeit down-market and small-time, commercial area into a mess of derelict shop-fronts and dark alleyways where drug-pushers plied their trade and prostitutes flaunted their wares. A pub here and a bank there picked up the pennies and the pounds of the black economy, and a bookshop held on like faith for better days to come. But the only auguries for the future were the desultory Portakabins that the police set up from time to time to clear the streets for the tourists.

Lindiwe knew most of the street dwellers by sight and would pass them by with a nod and a smile. Anything more familiar was not called for, and assistance of any sort was taboo – from the locals, anyway. The tourists were another matter, and the American hotel at the more respectable end of King's Cross made sure that there was a steady supply of those.

Most of the others at the Centre were afraid to walk to the station alone after dark, but Lindiwe floated along without a fear in the world. This was her patch, her little jungle and she knew it well, knew its dangers and was unafraid. It was no more dangerous than the slums of her native Johannesburg, in which she had grown up and would be living still, but for the grace of God and the Bishop of Soweto, who had got her a scholarship to study abroad. As it was, she had escaped to

England and freedom, but she still looked back over her shoulder at those she felt she had abandoned. And, although she sent money to her parents, living sparingly herself, and her work at the Centre enabled her to channel funds to the townships back home, she could not overcome the sense of guilt she felt at being the fortunate one. She should be there, working on the ground, her ground, the ground she knew so well, not fobbing off the job with grants to well-meaning outsiders who had no feel for the people or their problems. She had thought she could be of use to the denizens of King's Cross, but there was nothing she could do for them: they had gone beyond despair into an underworld of their own.

But this man who followed her, he did not belong here, above ground or below, neither tourist nor denizen. He was too shabbily dressed for one and too long in the tooth for the other; no one on the street lived long enough to grow that old.

He was sixty, if he was a day, thought Lindiwe, and looked the very image of a dirty old man – tall and stooped, in a crumpled old raincoat and a battered felt hat, staring short-sightedly at the pimps and the prostitutes from under the faded awning of the bookshop. That was why Lindiwe had noticed him when she had gone in to buy a book for her godmother: the stereotype was too flagrant to be missed. She saw him there the following day, and off and on for the next two weeks in the run-up to Christmas, at four o'clock of an evening, when the winter light was fading and Lindiwe was hurrying home.

Then he disappeared altogether, and Lindiwe had all but forgotten him when, on a cold February day, she saw him follow her all the way to the Centre. But, when she turned round at the door, he had gone. She did not see him again for a while after that, but, about two weeks later, she found him following her again, at a distance at first, but closer and closer as the days went by – till, one morning, she found him at the door of the Centre, waiting for it to open.

"What is it you want?" Lindiwe burst out, shocked out of her usual kindliness, and the man, startled, managed to stammer out, "I, I . . . Sorry" in a high-pitched voice before he turned on his heels and fled.

Lindiwe slammed the door behind her and, picking up the mail, took it into Mr Admad's office, to find that the director had already come in.

"What on earth is the matter, Lindiwe?" asked Ahmad, as she handed him the post. "You look angry and displeased."

"It's this man, boss," Lindiwe sank into the visitor's chair across Ahmad's desk. "I am sure he is following me. A shabby old man –"

"Ah, the chap who was hanging around, watching all those people."

"Oh yes. I told you about him, didn't I? I am sure he means no harm. Not that I am afraid of him or anything." Her eyes lit up with battle.

"No, I should say not," laughed Ahmad, looking at Lindiwe's portly figure. "Your walk alone is enough to frighten anyone."

"But he's weird. There's something not right there." Lindiwe lit a cigarette and Ahmad pushed the ashtray towards her. "There's a, there's a . . . what is that saying of yours?"

"Which one?" inquired Ahmad uneasily. Lindiwe was always teasing him about his colonial education and his fondness for proverbs and quotations.

"You know . . . when something is not right and you feel it. A sort of out-of-tune thing."

"A rift in the lute, you mean," offered Ahmad carefully.

"That is it, a rift in the lute, that is the feeling I get every time I see him. Uneasy, that's what I am, uneasy." Lindiwe stubbed out her cigarette and rose to go. "Don't worry, boss, it will pass. Or he will," she added with a guffaw.

"I have no doubt about that, Lindiwe. There's nothing and no one you cannot handle."

A week later, Lindiwe came up to Ahmad's desk, all flushed and flustered.

"It's that man again, boss. I could not mistake that squeaky voice of his. On the phone."

"What man?"

"You know, the old fellow I told you about? Who was following me?"

"Ah, him. On the phone? What does he want?"

"Oh, he wanted to know about the changes in our organization – whether we are still a charity and, if so, how could we bring out such a controversial paper like *Power and Poverty*. Weren't we afraid of being closed down? That sort of thing. Do you want to speak to him?"

"Did he ask for me?" inquired Ahmad, "I mean, did he want somebody in authority? Is he that type of man?"

"No, he didn't, not really. But he is funny. Wanted to know how we publish things, run a library and hold meetings, all on a staff of three or four. Things like that. I told him we had volunteers, and then he questions that. How do we get them? Why do they volunteer? When I replied that they probably find our work now speaks to their problems, he paused a long while and said, 'Oh, I see.' Funny man. Could be anything, a nutter or a National Front guy, or someone from the Charity Commission, spying on us after that article in the *Mail*."

"Well, don't keep him hanging on. Be guarded in what you say and try to find out what he really wants. Why not ask him directly? Or tell him to come and see us. We can assess him better then."

"Yes, all right, if you say so," condescended Lindiwe and sashayed out of the room. She came back a few minutes later.

"Did you find out anything more?" Ahmad queried.

"I told you, he is mad. When I asked him about him and what he did, he went off on a long tale about how he was in a similar position as ourselves. I don't know what he means except that he is broke and wants money – wants to give us money, too, but hasn't any. And then he asked for suggestions as to how he could get some 'untainted' funds, yes untainted was the word he used, for his own work, work with people he said. He had heard that we had broken with big business and industry and had no money, and yet had managed to survive. 'Carry on'," Lindiwe mimicked the man's high nasal tone, "'carry on the good work'. I am sure he is a nut, or he has been put up by somebody to check on us."

"You are beginning to develop a siege mentality," Ahmad reproached her gently. "Is he going to come in?"

"Yes, that's the only way I could get rid of him. And you had better see him when he comes. I've had enough . . ."

On the following Monday, Lindiwe accosted Ahmad in the corridor.

"You just missed him," she said. "He was passing this area, he said, and dropped in. I spoke to him at the door – I was going to the bank – and got rid of him quickly. He is coming in next week, though. That man I was telling you about," she added, as Ahmad looked blankly at her. "You know, the nut who wanted to know about our Centre, made all those inquiries the other day."

"Oh yes," nodded Ahmad, "that guy. Good. I'll see him when he comes."

Four days later, Lindiwe stormed into Ahmad's room.

"He is here, he is here," she said in an agitated whisper, "that mad man –"

"Show him in," interrupted Ahmad.

A large shabby man with greying hair and a stoop, ruddy-complexioned, coat and hat in hand, walked in after Lindiwe.

Ahmad looked up from his desk and rose quickly from his chair with both arms outstretched, ignoring Lindiwe's clandestine warnings to be discreet.

"Reverend John Fortune," he greeted the man, "how nice to see you. Please sit down."

Lindiwe was aghast.

"We met, I think, some years ago at the World Council of Churches' consultation on racism. 1969? My name is Ahmad."

The old man was shaken, moved. Someone had recognized him.

"I have read your books, of course," continued Ahmad and, turning to Lindiwe, he said, "Mr Fortune worked among the hill tribes of India for over twenty years, taught them, helped them, fought their battles with them against the government. Of course he was thrown out. You should read his . . ."

John Fortune had slumped into his chair. He had let the mass of him slacken in a heap. Lindiwe reached out to help him, but he waved her aside. "Thirty years," he said, but not in a tone of regret. "Thirty years," he repeated, rubbing his hands as though to warm himself in the glow of remembered days. But then there was Independence and things had begun to change. He had thought he could do missionary work in his own country, but they didn't want people like him any more, they had the police instead. He smiled to himself, a sad smile, wry. There were tears behind his thick glasses somewhere, they had misted over.

"What could be worse," he asked Ahmad, "than a missionary without a mission?" And then he smiled that smile of his again and added, "unless it is a mission without a missionary?"

The following week, Lindiwe came up to Ahmad and put a letter in his hand, "I am going home to Africa," she said.

A Family Man

Fern Spitzer

On a Monday morning in November of 1979, after twenty-two long and boring years as a drugged and subdued psychiatric patient, Jimmy Lindsay was being discharged from Friern Barnet Hospital. He had completed three months in rehab, lessons in how to fry or boil an egg, peel a potato, open a tin, etc. etc. etc. – all the things his wife could do for him. Then, at the end of the course, two nurses came over to shake his hand and wish him well, saying they imagined how happy he must be feeling. Yes, he was glad he was leaving – after all they had done to him – but he wasn't happy. How could he feel happy with this big hard lump in his chest? A lump of stuck memories. Like the time in the workshop when he had complained that the white instructor was teaching them wrong. They grabbed him from behind and injected him. Said he was shouting and threatening. It wasn't true. But that's how he learned it was better to say nothing. Years and years of saying nothing.

The social worker who came to the ward to collect him was a delicate slip of a thing with straight blonde hair and a jittery smile. Young, probably about twenty-five years old. Her name was Sally Hill.

They passed Reception and walked out of the large Victorian brick building into a cold murky day. The thick grey mist hung over Jimmy, pressing down on his shoulders and tightening his breathing. He was carrying a battered leather suitcase half-filled with a few articles of clothing and toiletries and a framed copy of his wedding photograph, wrapped in a towel to keep it from getting scratched. No baby pictures. He didn't know what had happened to them, when they had gone missing. The hospital was a place where things got lost.

His own clothes, lost. Most of his discharge outfit came from the second-hand shop – good grey trousers, not-so-white shirt, and a paisley tie with a small grease stain near the bottom. The smart tweed jacket was given to him by a nurse, who said that her husband would never be that slim again. Socks and underwear were new, courtesy of social services or the hospital, he wasn't sure which.

"This way, my car is over here," the social worker said.

Jimmy looked down at his wedding ring on the hand clutching the suitcase. What the social worker told him last week didn't make sense. How could he be divorced? Jasmine would never do anything like that, go behind his back and make up lies. She was a sweet loving woman and he had never done anything wrong, never got drunk, never raised a hand to her – he could swear it on a Bible.

"You can put your suitcase on the back seat. Sorry about the mess, just slide the books and things over." She held open the door of her red Volkswagen Polo.

Where were they going? Who was he supposed to be, dressed in clothes shaped by another man's body? The front of the car felt cramped. He pulled back his knees and leaned towards the door, away from the social worker. She was still too close. He felt invaded by her flowery scent and the tinkle of her dangling earrings.

"You really are lucky we managed to find you such a nice flat," she said.

He nodded and continued staring out of the window as the car moved through the North London traffic. At first he didn't recognize the streets, but then, when they passed the Archway and started down Holloway Road, things began to look familiar.

"Your flat has been freshly painted and has central heating and a small fitted kitchen. It's near the Angel." She stopped at a red light and glanced over at her silent passenger. "Do you remember that part of Islington?" she asked.

"Sort of," he said, not really sure what her question meant. He watched a large-boned Caribbean woman bend over a pushchair to adjust a child's woollen hat, her coat stretched tight over solid hips. A shiver went through his body. The woman looked so like Jasmine that he wanted to call out to her.

"I hope you won't feel lonely, what with the day centre and the people there." She signalled a turn. "When we get to your flat I'll show you where the bus stop is – it's a number thirty-eight."

"Miss, may I ask you something?" he asked.

"Yes, certainly. And you can call me Sally."

"Sally." He considered her name.

"Yes." She waited.

"Do you know where my son Daniel is?"

"I'm sorry it's taking so long – the traffic is quite bad today – but we should be there in about twenty minutes. We can talk then."

He slumped back. The image of the child in the pushchair became Daniel, laughing and waving chubby little arms. Jimmy longed for the hugs of his baby son. In spite of the problems with money, those were the good years. He didn't know what had happened. What had caused his life to change into this sad emptiness? Why had he been locked up? The day they took him away – a scramble of people he'd never met, two police, a social worker and a doctor – no one explained the laws. When he tried to talk they injected him.

Over the years the medication and bad food had brought him down. He wanted to get back to his old self, to step into a body which stood up straight. To think clearly. But his mind kept doing strange things; long ago seemed like yesterday and yesterday was already lost. He could not remember the name of the street they were headed for, where he would be living.

Inside the flat the social worker showed him around. There was a bedroom, bathroom, sitting room and kitchen. Small and plain. She had bought tea bags, milk and sugar.

"Have you used an electric kettle before?" she asked.

"Yes, in rehab," he answered, glancing across at the dull green wall. Did Jasmine still live in the flat with the bright yellow kitchen?

The social worker pulled the chairs back from the table. Jimmy sat opposite and took a sip of tea to calm his voice. He spoke quietly. "Do you know where Daniel is?"

"Daniel is fine. He's a grown man now. Married and has a job. That's all I know. I've never met him, but have been told he's doing well."

"I'm glad to hear that," he said, hanging his head. His eyes looked blank, the crying was inside his chest – crying for all he had missed.

Sally took out a pad and pen and explained that they needed to make a list of what to buy for the flat. "You'll need a rubbish bin, and a draining rack in the kitchen. Anything else you can think of?"

A bird. Jasmine had embroidered the most beautiful bird imaginable. The wings were made up of different shades of crimson and gold. Hundreds of tiny little stitches. "No, I can't think of anything," he said.

The social worker added a few more items, put the pen down and looked across at Jimmy's sad face. She smiled nervously. "Mr Lindsay, your son Daniel is fine. I know that when he was a baby you used to worry someone was trying to kidnap him, but that was part of your illness."

No. What she had been told was wrong. The words he had heard coming through the walls were real. The neighbours whispering, plotting to steal his bright-eyed infant son. The knife was to scare them off . . . nothing more.

"I'm glad that he is fine now," Jimmy said.

At the door she shook his hand and wished him well in his new home.

* * *

The first few months of life outside the hospital passed quickly. During the week Jimmy spent mornings at the day centre and afternoons in the betting shops, alternating between Ladbrokes and Graham Taylor, Turf Accountants. The day centre mornings were all right. They had art and music and that sort of thing. It wasn't hard and no one bothered him if he didn't feel like doing much.

After lunch, on his way out, one of the friendly staff usually asked, "Are you coming to the group this afternoon?"

Jimmy said yes, meaning no. He was off to the betting shop.

When he got there it was, "How goes it, mate?"

"Not too bad."

No big conversations. No personal questions. It was an easy relaxing place. He watched the others and tried to figure where luck was – if it was his turn for a win. Sometimes, if things felt wrong, he didn't bet at all.

Weekends he stayed in, day-dreamed the days away and thought about painting the walls a colour Jasmine would like. But never got around to it.

One Thursday afternoon, after weeks and weeks of bad luck, Jimmy finally had a win. Enough to buy some toys for his children. He went to Woolworth's and bought a fluffy little bear, a doll's tea service, a bus and a fire engine, crayons, paints and a pad of coloured paper. All the things they liked.

The following morning he carried the two bulging shopping bags to his appointment with his social worker and placed them on her desk. "Can you give these things to my children?" he asked.

"I'm sorry," she said. "Your children are all grown up."

As soon as the words were out of her mouth he realized his mistake. He sometimes saw things which weren't there. Not ghosts. More like television pictures of his memories.

Yesterday, when he passed a playground, he saw his children. Alice, Yvette, Amelia, Patricia and Daniel. But when he went over to talk to them they ran away, shouting, 'You're not our daddy'.

The girl in the newsagent's resembled Jasmine. The tilt of her head and the way she pinned back her hair. A polite girl who always said good morning and thank you, when he bought his newspaper.

He did not know how to explain to Sally that part of him understood but that, at times, it felt better not to know.

"Are there any children in one of those social services homes who might like some toys? You could give them these."

"Thank you," she said. "That's very generous of you."

"Do you know where they are, my wife Jasmine, and my children? Even if they are grown up . . . "

She shook her head. "Sorry. I can't help."

Sally meant that about him being generous. He was a tender-hearted soul, but there was nothing she could do. She didn't know how to explain the situation without adding to his hurt.

For the rest of their meeting Jimmy nodded, yes, fine, to all of her questions, waiting for the final "Anything else?"

"No thank you, miss."

"I guess that's it, then. I'm pleased you're doing so well."

* * *

By June, his first free after-hospital summer, he became bored with the day centre programme – all that art, music, movement and drama stuff. It was childish, nothing to help him get a job and earn money. He decided to skip the groups, but didn't want to miss the lunch. Particularly as the new cook sometimes made chicken with rice and red peas. So he began spending his mornings at Ladbrokes and afternoons at Graham Taylor, fitting in a meal at the day centre in between.

As he was getting up from the table, Naomi, one of the staff, slid into the chair opposite him. "Before you go, I'd like to have a word with you," she said.

Jimmy sat back down.

"You've stopped coming to the groups."

"Yes," he answered.

"Are you all right?"

"Yes."

"Can you tell me . . . ?"

He noticed a few grey hairs in her dark curls and thought her brown eyes had a sympathetic look. "I like the betting shops," he said.

"I don't understand."

"I like the feeling of winning. There's nothing like it. Sometimes you almost win, you're so close that your heart starts pounding. But then, when you do win – well, that's it. It's so good you can't stop smiling."

"I'm not sure . . . "

"You could come with me and try it sometime . . . " He lifted his eyebrows.

The note of flirtation startled her. "I just wanted to know how you are," she said.

"Fine, I'm fine."

She decided to let it drop. As long as he wasn't spending the day in bed he was probably coping with his depression.

After the betting shop Jimmy went back to his fourth floor flat. The air was stifling. He opened the cold water taps in the kitchen and bathroom to cool the place down. Settled into his armchair and began reading the *Mirror*. Lulled by the steady gush of running water, his eyes closed and the newspaper slid to the floor. His head flopped, waking him with a jolt. He looked around the room, checking that it was not the hospital ward. Got up and fried an egg and made tea and toast. The same lonely supper. It was all right if you were a loner. There were quite a few of those around the day centre. But he was a family man, not meant to eat and sleep alone.

* * *

His September appointment with the social worker got off to a bad start. She told him that the landlord had complained about the running water.

"Couldn't you just open a window?" she asked.

"How does he know about the water? He can't hear it."

"We've talked about this before."

"I don't like spies. How is it my own flat if I'm being spied on?" He watched her write something and knew that he had said the wrong thing. To all her other questions – How are you getting on at the day centre? Are you managing to keep your flat tidy? Have you seen the nurse for your injection? – he answered with a silent nod.

When he got home he filled the kettle and left the water running. While the kettle was boiling he went into the bathroom, had a pee, washed his hands, turned off the hot and left the cold. He reached over and opened the cold water in the bath, making sure that it was on full force. He needed the running water to let some air in – to keep him from suffocating.

Even in the middle of the afternoon the sitting room was dark. His single armchair, with day centre brown stripes, was too small for his six-foot body. Jimmy stretched his legs forward, heels on the floor, pushing his backside against the chair back, trying to massage the injection sore spot. As the medication began to blur his brain he drifted to bumping along on the patty pan going out of Kingston. He was on his way to Industry Village to visit the teenage Jasmine, who lived with her grandma in rooms above a shop. To ask her to come walk by the river. Listen to the flow of water. See the small pink flowers. The Blue Mountains. It was all so clear.

He needed to find her and take her back to that river where she would be able to hear what he was asking. He was asking her. Her, the one he wanted, the pretty girl with the matching name. Jasmine. Jasmine and Jimmy.

For hours he dozed off and came to, back and forth, dipping into his youth in Jamaica and coming back to try to make sense of his life here in London. He needed to get a job, to earn money, to find Jasmine, to ask her . . . The problem was his brain. It kept going fuzzy. The paths were overgrown. He got lost in the tangles and couldn't find his way.

* * *

It was now more than a year since his hospital discharge. Another dreary English winter. Day after day of grey skies, relentless rain. A bad luck time. Jimmy decided to leave off Ladbrokes and return to the day centre mornings. They had started a writing group. Naomi asked him if he would like to give it a try.

"I didn't have much time at school. Will you help me with my spelling?" he asked.

"Sure, that's OK."

"Will you help me to write about my home? I want to write something for my children."

"That's a good idea," she said.

The group of eight patients sat around a table. Jimmy wrote a few words which he did not want anyone to see. "Can I take this away?" he asked.

He opened the notebook on his kitchen table and stared down at the lined paper. In his mind he saw vivid pictures and puzzled over how to form a likeness using the letters of the alphabet. Every day he wrote, pressing down hard on his pencil, adding more words – sometimes six or seven, others only one or two. He carried his notebook everywhere to catch the words which popped up. To catch them before they faded.

His luck began to change. A few small wins. A couple of pints at his local. He was on the right track. He could feel it – this was the beginning of something. He was going to get there.

The weather improved. The days became lighter. It was warm enough to go around without an overcoat. England was almost nice.

He was back in the routine of day centre mornings. A cloud inside his head had lifted and things began to make sense. The painting sessions were peaceful. On his way from the centre he hummed a tune to Lady Luck. He could tell his turn was coming soon – *Luck be a lady tonight.*

The week before Easter, he was in Graham Taylor's, notebook in one hand, betting slip in the other. It could be today. It could be today. The words kept going through his head. Let it be today. As the winner was announced he held his breath . . . And it is Jennifer Dee, the winner is Jen-ni-fer Dee. His heart leapt and his chest expanded. Finally, his big win.

"Good one, mate." The regulars clapped him on the shoulder.

The next day he followed his plan. Went straight to the Burton Menswear shop on Oxford Street and selected a light beige suit, two white shirts, a beige and cream striped tie, socks, shoes and underwear. The suit was made of fine Italian wool. Standing in front of the full-length mirror he turned to see how the jacket fell – not a ripple; it fit perfectly. He stroked the sleeve, feeling the soft material. This was definitely the right suit. With shoulders thrust back, head held high, he smiled at his handsome image. Looking like this he could go anywhere in the world.

The salesman hovered. "Excuse me, sir. How will you be paying? Cheque or credit card?"

"Huh. What are you saying? I don't get your meaning, man."

"Excuse me, I was just asking about your method of payment."

"I ain't no thief. I am paying with good English money. The Queen and all. Look at that. Does that answer your question, man?"

The salesman folded the clothes, inserting layers of tissue paper.

On his way home Jimmy stopped off at Marks and Spencer and bought a pound of large green grapes. He looked at the bunches of flowers. The deep red tulips were splendid. Jasmine liked red, but he wasn't sure how well they would keep. Better to buy them tomorrow.

In his flat he rinsed the grapes and placed them on a plate. Never once in all his hospital years or at the day centre did they give the patients grapes. Didn't they know that fruit was healthy? He wrote 'grapes' and 'tulips' in his notebook. Two nice words.

Before going to bed he took a long hot bath and in the morning dressed in his new suit.

At the day centre the patients oohed and aahed and wanted to know where he was going. Naomi blushed and told him he looked wonderful.

The Graham Taylor regulars couldn't believe how terrific Jimmy looked.

"Hey, Jimmy man, what's happening? Your daughter getting married or something?"

"Not exactly," he said.

"That sure is one swell suit."

He breathed in the warm compliment.

When Jimmy went out that evening, still finely dressed, he was carrying his notebook and a large bunch of red tulips. For hours he walked up and down the streets of North London trying to find the block of flats where they used to live. Some things had changed. There were buildings he'd never seen before. He couldn't find the corner shop. He wasn't sure where he was.

It was past midnight when he was stopped by two policemen. Both tall, about the same height as Jimmy, but one was a bit fat. The hefty one asked him what he was doing staring up at the windows of a house in the middle of the night. They wanted to know what was in the notebook.

"The notebook is for me to write my life," Jimmy explained. "I've lost my life and I am trying to find it. My wife lives in one of these houses, but I don't know which one."

"Do you mean you've lost your key?" the slim one asked.

"No, I don't have a key. Please, can you help me find her?"

In the end they couldn't figure out what the problem was. The words in his notebook didn't make sense. They weren't sure whether his wife existed. He seemed to be saying that he hadn't seen her for more than twenty years. He wasn't drunk but he did sound confused. They took him to the police station and contacted social services. Yes, the Islington night duty team recognized the name and would send someone to deal with the situation.

The social worker they sent was a skinny young man in torn jeans and a crumpled T-shirt. He sat across from Jimmy and pulled his chair in, scraping it across the hard floor. He came so close that his frayed denim knee almost touched the crease in Jimmy's trousers.

"Jimmy, Mr Lindsay. I know that you do not like what I am telling you, but are you listening?"

Jimmy's eyes fixed on the tear in the jeans – pale skin showing through a pattern of loose threads.

The social worker raised his voice. "Do you understand what I am saying?"

He knew he could not trust any of them. If he spoke out they might lock him up again.

"Are you listening? Are you taking anything in?"

Why should he listen to more lies?

"I need you to look up at me." He waited. "I need to see your face to know that you are listening."

Jimmy raised his head.

"You have to accept the fact that Mrs Lindsay is no longer your wife. You have to stop looking for her. She does not want to see you."

His head dropped back down, eyes closed. As the bus swerved around the bend, over the gorge, Jimmy could feel the warmth of her hand in his, holding on.

Myself When I Am Real

James Fellows

SW11

Miles' lower lip was the first in the silent classroom to quiver. He stretched his jumper sleeves hurriedly down over his hands. It made the ends go really saggy but this way he felt safe. Like when he used to put clocks down the toilet to keep bedtime away. And when the ends were saggy, he could look up them and store things in there if he wanted to. It was the same place where the toothpaste juice went when he did his teeth before bed. Down the toothbrush, through his fingers, under his watch and along to his elbow, where it fell off. A little knob of runny toothpaste on a mission. like a toboggan. Sometimes his arm smelled minty the next day and he could see the white track it had left that was a bit like chalk on the board that Misdrake didn't rub off properly because she was looking the other way. Waving at the board but not looking at it. Waving at the board but looking at us, her mouth opening and closing with words falling out. It was clever that she could do that, those two different things at the same time, waving and talking. She was a clever lady and Miles loved her very much.

When he was older and had more hair, they would walk around together with square bags, holding hands, and when it was her birthday, he would give her the mobile that was the same pink colour as her ears when she was happy. The pink 'phone was in the shop on the way to school and he looked in the window every morning to check it was still there. Sometimes he walked to the shop on Saturday as well, just because you never know. Sundays were OK because people only bought food and newspapers on Sundays and sometimes clothes. The best thing would be to buy it now and save it but it was too much money and it might start ringing and then people would know.

But Misdrake, sitting at the front of the class, had just put her glasses on and Miles wanted to cry because it meant she had Something Serious to Say. He knew that the others wanted to cry too because Shashona sitting in front of him was playing with her fuzzy hair-worms. Leyla, the girl who followed Misdrake around the classroom with a dustpan and brush, looked upset as well. She was flatting down with both hands the front of the funny potato-colour wedding dress she wore to school but it kept jumping back up like there were small birds inside. Miles wanted to sniff his favourite smell, the special smell that lived under the watch. If he kept his watch on for a long time the smell got better. It wasn't always a nice smell like petrol stations or the smell of the tube train coming but it was his secret smell. He looked down at his watch, the place where the smell started but all he could see was a black sleeve-stump.

Special smell *or* safety sleeves? Couldn't have both.

It was hard to know.

They had wanted to cry in Misdoolan's class too, the children, because she had said that our lungs could go round the world more than once. Miles gazed out of the window at the greenery that had been fenced out of the playground. He thought hard about caterpillars and *the change* because he didn't want to think about lungs.

At break, the boys had had a special meeting behind the electricity substation at the back of the school, to talk about this, about lungs. Miles knew that at the meeting it was good to say important things and use special words and not spit. They would try to decide what to do to stop their lungs from going around the world because without lungs you can't smoke. Some of the boys weren't sure if they wanted to smoke but it was nice to have the choice.

SW2

"You won't believe what happened today, Salim! Can you pass the ashtray? You know my lenses, no, no, the other one there next to the lamp. Mmm. Empty it, would you? My lenses have been stinging, *really* stinging this week, so I decided not to wear them today, saves time in the morning too and I need to get my prescription checked anyway. My eyeball is oval like an egg, *astigmatic*, and the shape can change over time."

I stopped listening to the words, which hung in the room like wallpaper, just a moment ago. We are sitting so close, perched on the corner of her bed, that I can smell her breath, the vessel upon which her words are borne, and it is astonishingly good, comforting, like airing cupboards in British households. Every few moments a volley of bibs and parps rises up from the din of late rush hour vehicles passing below and is answered with a brief frown from Emily, formed without her knowing. It is still quite light in her spacious orange bedroom although the day is beginning to gather in its skirts. It will be some hours yet 'til the gentle contours of the face I have loved touching fall into a silhouette. And we will sit and talk until darkness erases us from the room, makes us equal, if I have my way.

Emily loves me quite as I am, which is the problem and is driving me away from her. She doesn't see me the way her parents, friends, colleagues do. She doesn't insist that I work to belong, doesn't understand that I should have to mute my otherness to fit in. And that's what drew me to her, the acceptance in her embrace that is warm like a murmur forgotten in sleep. From the way she yielded to the first lingering touch of my dark-slender fingers at her creamy nape, I sensed that one day I would revolt against her kindness.

"I was sitting at my desk. Have you got a lighter? Mmm, and the moment I put my glasses on, no that one doesn't work, the children started crying! Can you believe it? The matches'll do, there, no, by the picture frame. It was the little Jamaican boys first, the ones who do the crotch-grabbing dancing in the playground and ask if they can 'sex me up'. It's not lit, mmm, and one of them piped up, Jamal, I think, in a really thin voice, 'please take them off Miss, we're sorry', and the whole class started nodding. Hilarious!"

And as she breathes out this memory, smiling inwardly in her way, I am struck by the grace with which she taps the ash into the ashtray which is on the floor. Each move in this simple sequence is precise but effortless and as she bends down, the shadowy tumbling coils of her hair part to reveal the whiteness of her nape. And I think that even at her most sophisticated she shows me, in turning away, her nakedness.

This is Emily when she is real.

To break the seduction, I tell her about Faisal and his observations.

"When he's waiting for a bus and an unsavoury type turns up, y'know, a mumbler or a crazy, he notices how the people around him sort of stiffen up: fists clench and jaws clamp, they shuffle and puff and look at their wrists. This happens, apparently, not because they're frightened or disgusted by the freak but because, according to Mr Anthropology, *they wish to take him into their hearts, yeah, but are prevented from doing so because of social pressures to exclude weirdoes.* I'm quoting him."

Emily is crooked at the mirror now, wiping the day from her face with balls of cotton wool, examining with keen interest the filth that has been worried loose. A single spotlight is trained on the mirror and peals of confused light bounce off it back into the room, disorientated. Without losing eye contact with herself, she flicks the cotton wool ball towards the corner of the room where it comes to rest amongst other wayward missiles that huddle like offerings before the bin.

"So our man Faisal, the supreme arbiter, makes a point of engaging the newcomer in lively, topical chat and the people breathe a sigh of communal relief and even throw smiles in his direction like they're throwing bouquets at his feet. This, he reckons, is because he has taken the role of *group ambassador* and in inviting the stranger to join in, he *breaks the myth of otherness, yeah, that society has created to cripple integration.* The bus stop is now a riot of warm feeling."

I don't think she is listening to me. Our words have become like blinkered horses galloping towards each other from separate shores, without breaking their stride even when they meet. Like dirty cotton wool balls that fall short of their target. I can feel the anger rising quickly, the anger of her back to me.

"It's such bollocks. He's a bloody other too! As welcome in this culture as the stinking tramp. Fuck! All this crap about being a group ambassador. Doesn't he see that he isn't part of the set-up in this country, he's just about tolerated as long as he keeps his head down and doesn't mess with things?"

"Sal*eeeeeem*! What is it with you? How can you still think this way? You're so deluded."

She has her back to her reflection and the light now, which makes her edges glow. So pure, this one. She stands, one hand on one hip, between me and the second-hand brightness, squeezing her exasperation into the cotton wool ball.

I am darker than ever.

"Whatever. Anyway, Faz says all this has *really positive implications, yeah.*"

We've been here, at this distant but timetabled outpost, many times before. This time, though, neither of us wants to pause and stretch our legs, probe through our considerable baggage. The hum of traffic outside has waned almost totally and I think I can hear threads of her affection straining. She is relieved that I have whatevered my way away from our grief but I can sense a new weariness as she humfs curtly back to the light of her reflection and whispers to herself, flatly, undressed of feeling, the way she reads aloud, to my embarrassment, from subtitled films at the cinema.

"I get so tired of this."

"Faz says", I continue, undeterred, voice rising, "says that this logic may also work on the tube and that – and this is the biggy – perhaps if one person gives to a beggar or even *fumbles around for loose change with the intent of giving,* everybody will follow suit! Ha! And this would happen of course, of course, because, wait for it, *the instinct to give to the impoverished, yeah, has been validated by such an act when performed by a member of a social group, yeah, with whom the majority can identify,* or something. Arise Faisaliji, shatterer of castes! And this, you see . . ."

"Salim. Please stop," she whispers.

A cool hand on a feverish brow.

A rubber brake pad on a wildly wheeling wheel.

From the fruit bowl in the kitchen, she carries in two bananas and a clementine and tucks them into my satchel on top of last week's shattered lychees and passion fruit.

Something for tomorrow's lunch.

I don't even like fruit.

N1

Through a tangle of tunnels that spreads its spindly limbs beneath the over-ground concerns of the city, a snub-nosed train rattled away like a loose part. Slumped in his seat on a train that pummelled its way blindly back and forth, a man with an empty record bag studied the colours that came together uneasily in the upholstery before him. It was an unhappy marriage of olive, puce and violet that had worn pale in places through the passage of time and the relentless see-sawing of buttocks and thighs that accompanied it. As he looked around the carriage, he could find only suggestions of its human freight. In the greasy marks on the windows where lolling heads had rested and the burnished silver footprints that gathered impatiently about the sliding doors there were echoes of life. But echoes were not what he was after today. He was here to influence, for the greater good, patterns of human behaviour and response and to liberate the instinct of generosity. What were the tools of this inquiry? Why, just a trouser pocket large enough to accommodate an earnest rifling and a watchful eye. And, of course, he needed passengers either seated or standing and a shabby vagrant with a spirit sufficiently broken for all pride to have seeped away.

Moments later the tube train swept open its doors to a crush of intent public. In the general kerfuffle, Faisal didn't see him get on but as the crowd thinned out and bodies slunk into their seats, there emerged by the doors a windswept young man, dowdy and blinking in stained clothes. He resembled a book that had been thumbed over and again by its reader, and wore an edge of bewildered surprise, dark hair sprouting off in all directions. Rubbing his crinkled hands together, the vagrant prepared his requests. Faisal gulped, his sizeable Adam's apple riding up and down, because he knew the time was now. time to put theory into practice.

Alighting from the train twenty minutes later and eight carriages from where he and the beggar (now considerably wealthier) had got on, Faisal did a sort of victory jig. Hunkered down, arms clamped tightly to his sides like chicken wings, he swivelled at the hips from left to right balancing on one foot and then the other and pounded on an imaginary drum.

His guesses had proved dead right. Pukka, in fact. But this was just the top of the iceberg, he reflected, as he threaded his hurried way out of the Underground, head down, leaving behind the staccato of shunting train traffic that bounced more distantly now off the curving tiled walls of the station like fading applause. It was time to apply what he had learned and to do this he would need an accomplice. Salim knew and had dissed his ideas from the get-go, so hung up on passing people by at high speed, with getting away from contact, even more now since he split with his lady. He'd grown cold and distant and was always angry, wouldn't admit that he missed her tenderness and that the missing was driving him wild.

Yeah, Salim needs to be part of this, to get connected again. Needs some human contact, hugs and stuff. Your man's icing over, freezing his balls out in trying to belong.

Tomorrow. I'll call him tomorrow.

Early.

E12

I am too dark in my bedroom mirror and I was right to leave her. Leave her lazy acceptance of my otherness. I move back and forward in front of the mirror, watching my reflection loom and recede. The telephone is ringing downstairs. Dad'll get it. It's probably Emily. All these weeks on. This is one thing she can't seem to accept – that I no longer want to be with her.

"Sal. It's for you," his father calls from the downstairs phone. "Can you take it in your room?"

"Tell her I'm out", comes the reply.

Salim walks back towards the mirror and trips on the extension lead that runs from the phone socket in the hallway up into his bedroom. For a moment the cable is pulled taut, and upsets a cup of cold Assam tea that had been placed on it, on the hallway table where the phone cradle rests. The tea spills into the cradle but Salim's father doesn't notice.

"Sorry, dear, he's out. Why don't you try again later?" he says, and after a moment replaces the receiver into its cradle before edging awkwardly around the parked bicycle and into the living room.

There's tea in my ear again. Cold, wet and unwelcome Assam on this damp, weekday morning.

I take the phone, from which the tea seems to be leaking, away from my ear. The darkness of the hallway mutes the fading wallpaper scuffed black by resting cycles but I can still make out a slippery spread of post muffling the WELCOME doormat and the tea dripping from the telephone earpiece.

"You sleepin', Salim?" a voice percolates out of the phone.

Faisal knows he woke me, that I've been rising late, so he continues before waiting for my answer.

"Listen, mate, I put it into practice, yeah, theory into practice on the Undergound. Made some poor geezer's day. A bit of careful manipulation, yeah, and his pockets was full of spare change. Just needed a hand in liberating it, that's all."

As he speaks a glossy red takeaway leaflet slithers through the letter box, chased by a knot of cool air that draws goose pimples from my ankles.

I make my living couriering packages from one building to another. My preferred mode of transport is the bicycle, upon which I daily sluice the city's arteries, parrying the advances of oncoming traffic, whipping around docile double deckers that bob, big and stupid, in a sea of growling traffic. Tearing down an A-Z of alleys, banksides, conduits, courts and cuts, around circuses (Ludgate and Cambridge) and along mews, rows, wharfs and yards, I am an electrical impulse shot through the elaborate twinkling circuitry of the City. A-juddering and a-gargling up and down kerbs, working loose worries that fall from me like autumn leaves and away into the gutter, I bluster down streets. I am the wind in your hair, whooshing around corners, toppling the unwary.

Bearing silent witness to the snapping together of pieces in this multicultural puzzle of a city, I no longer celebrate diversity.

I know better. I've seen it all.

Seen the chilling yellow boards erected at crime scenes: *Did you see or hear anything? Can you help?* And the victims, always an ethnic of one sort or another, no doubt. I've seen the city's dark, shadowy minorities in huddles at bus shelters before dawn breaks. Night-bused up from Marcus Garvey Estate, Mahatma House, Tess Sanderson Way, to clean the colossal sky-scraping offices that grow taller still on an income of off-shore wealth. And as the light comes and the towering granite and glass blocks suck commuters out of trains and into their lifts and corridors, the ethnics are gone, leaving no trace but the stinging scent of disinfectant. Never to belong to the day or the city.

Each day I burn grooves deeper and deeper into the fabric of this place, yearning to outrun *my* native make-up, to be part of things, part of the light. Perhaps in turning the next corner, in jumping the next set of lights, I will shed this skin and finally, truly belong here.

"Listen, Sal." Faisal pauses, then resumes.

"I've been experimenting with them people on the Underground, yeah, and I'm right, they're itching to donate, just need a bit of encouragement. So you gotta give us a hand, with the next stage, I mean. We gotta open these people up, yeah, they're like, hiding from themselves."

Faisal also likes to hide himself.

Stocky in a fur-lined parka zipped up to a chin flecked with stubble that clings like iron filings and swarms densely about a jawline that provokes trust, he thinks he is handsome *in our Asian way*, a little gaunt, with a lingering intensity around the eyes. He wears camouflage trousers that single him out against the grey urban backdrop of the metropolis and carries an empty record bag. At times when we meet, Faisal holds back for a few moments so he can watch me waiting for him. In the echoing brightness of mainline stations, for example, he will observe me scanning the wordless press of figures that spills out of trains like dark paint from an upturned tin. Just watching. At these times, he catches expressions that he never knew belonged to me, were part of my repertoire. When he watches me from a distance in this way, he says, I am myself when I am real. Playing no role, I am alone and a little vulnerable and he can detect an openess in me that is mirrored by a quiet movement outwards in his own heart.

This is Faisal when he is real.

Always believing in the mystery of ordinary things, in some timeless truth that smoulders just beneath the surface of understanding.

In *fucking* foolishness.

I am now properly awake and the full extent of his naivety draws anger from me like the pin prick of a mosquito drawing blood.

"Faz, man, you're off your nut. Leave me out of this," I snap.

In the depths of my courier's satchel, beneath papers and packages, there lies fruit, withering and bruised, near composted. It's all that's left of what we had together, Emily Drake and I, a preserve of her past concern moistening the edges of urgent envelopes.

A chill has settled into the belly of things, and later today as I ride I have tears in my eyes, drawn out by the cycle courier's interface with the autumnal wind.

Nothing more.

N4

On account of the punch-drunk flocks of Arsenal fans, an occasional disorder of homesick Irishmen several sheets to the wind, and the music festivals in the nearby park, it was not unusual to hear singing in this unremarkable enclave of town. Otherwise, this was a place that people came to in order to go somewhere else. And dropped their litter while they waited.

Over the years it had hosted a high turnover of immigrant communities who had left their mark then gone up in the world, bequeathing their butchers and restaurants to future occupations. Its long-term residents, its lifers, had eventually given up trying to instil a sense of civic pride in the denizens who dropped in for a while. Giving up trying to make it chime in with certain advertising broadsheets' portrayals of a place that *would suit professional couple*, they instead endeavoured to make the most of the grime and chaos. To make a virtue of necessity. The mere progressive amongst them reversed its name with a wry chuckle, dubbing the place Krapy Rubsnif, and began to savour the whirligig of strange cultures that swept through the place like a sudden storm. The odd-shaped fruits that appeared in green grocers, silent women in burkhas who spat unexpectedly, the stench of exotic tobacco and the tangle of foreign tongues gave Krapy Rubsnif a thrilling edge that no amount of council regeneration projects had managed. And there were also smiles and belly laughs and extended families and *genuine concern* that reminded the young white professional Rubsniffers of something that had been lost. Or maybe just forgotten.

In keeping with the tenor of the place, Sayah was singing along to her little personal radio as she passed one of a family of squat blue-white newspaper sellers. A strange phenomenon, they dotted the city like immovable orphans with identical handwriting and called out "Evening's Started" even when it was only just lunchtime.

She had not been here, in this city, long, and had arrived with a small case, a daughter in a wedding dress and a head full of the nightmares of persecution. It wasn't until middle-age had sunk into her like a heavy varnish into rosewood that the long-coiled concern of a relative sprang her from an unlawful prison cell and pressed, with "get away!" eyes, a sheaf of notes and a moon-eyed daughter into her trembling hands. Into the slumbering darkness and the muezzin's first clattering call, she dragged herself and her wordless girl, through his holy exhortations that lit up the night like Scud missiles, out of the country and into a new life. And through the grace of The Almighty (The Indivisible, The Merciful), here she was, able to think about re-living an arrested youth, to sew up her sadness with threads of song and sing her way back into her prime.

Reverse into it like a trilling delivery van into a bakery.

Having been here just a matter of months, Sayah wasn't yet fluent in English, a language that soared over her head like a proud rainbow-coloured bird with secrets. But she knew about the English custom of making revolutions in the Happy New Year and would join hands with them, a new child in a playground game, by vowing to next year resolutions make the language her own. To fold it into the creases of her life like flour into dough. She had plans now.

A few verses ahead, on the same side of the road, her temporary home, hemmed in by plumper ones, hove into view. It stood, indifferent to her return, like a skinny customs officer forgotten by his superiors at a dusty border crossing. The melody quickly faded as, with a fresh flush of shame, she saw the white plastic supermarket bags hanging limply like forced confessions from every window ledge of the dirty-magnolia building. The bags sagged with cheese and milk and other perishables that would have been in the fridge, had fridges been provided in their rooms.

These were the flags of the displaced.

Sayah felt an ache of grief for the refugees with whom she shared the hostel. Like her, their destiny had been uncoupled from its native engine and rerouted through unfamiliar lands in which they were left to waft about like partially recalled memories. Like her, they had to broadcast their hasty transplantation from window ledges because a roof was more than *what you 'ad* and fridges were *listen you tekkin' the piss, lady?* Neither could they afford to dress their children for school. Their children, who had been quietly torn in so many secret places that fear had un-dimpled dimpled cheeks and uncurled freewheeling hair. Left it straight and responsible. Answerable to.

Instead of returning just yet the hostel, she walked on towards the newsagent up ahead on the opposite side of the road. She needed some sort of solace. Taped carelessly to the shop windows was a frieze of multi-coloured posters of alphabetically ordered country names, listed like an atlas-index of exiled nation states. Each shouted out Best Price, 30p per min, 25p per min, 28p per min to call home from beneath a swarm of exclamation marks. She would buy the cheapest phone card and call her husband's voice, which was all that remained of him back home, cheerfully giving directions on how to leave messages on his voicemail long after his body, punctured with the grief of interrogation, had been unceremoniously hanged from a date-palm tree that had belonged to her family for generations. The tree, tall and noble, had superintended the harmonizing of families in marriage and the celebrations of Id-ul-Adha and Id-ul-Fitr. it had fringed the edges of Sayah's growing up with its shady refuge, before bowing reluctant limbs to receive her husband's death.

But now they were at least safe, al-Hamdu Iillah (Gobby praised), and Hello Tahir, my Habibi, there are people here who tie bunches of flowers to lampposts and traffic lights, how lovely. And the roads tell you which way to look when you cross them. And there's a box on a park corner where you can sneak opinions freely, and . . .

Her little radio continued to rattle out its happy pop manifesto as she walked towards her purchase. Past a doddery borough bin disgorging its contents down its front like a drunk in a nodding stupor and busy red crisp packets whipped by the wind into a dervish-dance in the corner of a bus shelter.

Past mangled bike bits strapped to railings and telephone boxes upholstered with spread-eagled smut. Heavy trucks rumbled by, lashing her long skirts to her legs and piling her hair up at the back of her head with a wet *whoooooosheeeee.*

By and by, a cheery radio melody caught the downturn in her mood, offered her its hand and led her, singing, across the road.

In the drowsy afternoon air of the pub, a sleeping dog dreamed dog-dreams as his owner, leaning with a lusty glint into the bar to arm-wrestle the barmaid, inadvertently spilled ash onto his broad, furry head. A smoke haze hung thick and low around the drinkers like a dirty rumour. Pool balls clacked, the TV droned and a scream and the squeal of bicycle brakes from the street caused a disc of golden plantain to fall from a fork into a pint of Guinness. It rested a moment on the cushion of feathery froth like a copper coin before drowsily slinking out of view leaving a surprised “o” in its wake. The dog jerked up its head, dislodging the little ash pile and leaving a damp shiny dog muzzle outline on the tiled floor where it had rested.

“What in the Lord’s name . . .” a deep voice began, plucked from his musings about his son’s inquiries about lungs and their propensity to travel abroad.

“Can they, Dad, can lungs really travel?” he had asked in a voice that stood up on end like a new haircut as they sat together sharing in the end-of-day sitting room quiet.

“No, son. Your lungs can’t travel. Not without you, anyway.”

NW1–SE1–EC1–N4

It is well cold today but I am *so* fast, an extended essay in perpetual motion, stretching myself taut across a moving canvas of glossy tarmacadam, that I barely notice it. There is a fever growing inside me as I pass young men with old men's walking sticks, legs stretched out in front of them on graffitied benches, waving cans at passers-by. Past a barefoot Negro with a snake in a shopping trolley and a didgeridoo. From North to South then back again over loping bridges that squeeze traffic over the dark, rushing river, I lap menacingly around the edges of the city. Picking my way in and out of vehicles both stationary and moving, drawing alongside the latter able even to read the luminous chinks of the clocks on the dash, the twitchings of the speedometer – *fuck*, even the oil gauge – before sweeping silently into another slipstream, I defy belief. I am anonymity streamlined in helmet, mask and shades, one of the frenzied spawn of the fornicating city's dirty desire to cheat on distance, on the natural order of things, on time. I am its willing flunkey, its funky time-wallah, happily shorn of the twin decadences of patience and courtesy. Try to catch my shaded eye, to entreat me to spare you the terror of my passing (please, I'm elderly! I have a pram! you shouldn't be on the pavement!) and you will fail. Your smiles and scowls will never penetrate my courier's exhilarating livery.

You people, you *ped-est-ri-ans*, be warned, I am the fear that shivers your spine as you regain the safety of the kerbside, or step off a bus into my path, *The Wind In Your Hair, the-*

Chair legs scraped the pub floor with a woody rasping fart and pool tables and daytime TV were slowly abandoned as, one by one, the men peeled themselves away from their pleasures and massed at the window to find out *whappen?*

From his table in the window, Miles' father saw a woman kneeling in a gold-trimmed pool of long saffron skirts that seemed to be spreadng around her as though the fabric was leaking its pattern from a tear in the hem onto the road where she knelt.

An arabesque bleeding golden into the road.

Blasted cycle couriers, he cursed, never looking where they're going. Think they own the road. And now he's gone knocked over this lady. Looks like he came out worse, though. All the same, I'd give him what for, damn idiot.

But instead, in thee cornfield-folds of her lap, she cradled the head of the young man, whose helmet then sun-glasses she lifted gently off. He seemed to be crying.

"Yourself is hurt, isn't it?" Sayah, a little shaken but unhurt, asked, seeing the tears streaming behind his bruised and crooked sun-glasses, which she laid down beside him, unfolded.

"No," he moaned, trembling, touching the cool road. "I'm so . . ."

"Is all right", she whispered like a kiss, stroking his sad, dark hair.

". . . so sorry."

A small crowd of onlookers had gathered on the opposite side of the road. An elderly woman wearing a clear plastic headscarf, two burly men with multiple piercings holding hands and a sharply dressed young African with a mobile phone. The pensioner loosed the handle of her tartan shopping trolley and nudged the black man in the ribs who, after some hesitation, reluctantly broke away from the assembly, like a wasp leaving a hive, and offered his help.

N5–N15

"Excuse me for troubling you. I wouldn't ask if I weren't desperate."

Miles looked up from his Gameboy at the owner of the voice. Thumbs paddling away frantically, his roving eyes and pursed lips took in the features of the stray that had entered their busy carriage.

Lung thief?

He was certainly a stranger, called that 'cause he was stranger than other people you knew better. Scruffy man, hands dirty like he had been looking for worms, no shoelaces, nice teeth and a spensive watch he twisted roundandround like he was trying to screw his hand off. He carried a record bag.

Mustn't talk to him, Miles tutted, and thought of all the people he was stranger than as proof. Next to Miles sat a man, the same colour as the stranger, with a purple graze on his arm, wearing wonky sun-glasses. He seemed nervous, like a boy waiting for an in-jection from the school nurse. Very suspicious.

"I don't got no family or 'ome an' I bin sleepin' rough," the stranger than other people said digging his hands into his coat pockets and standing very still like he was waiting to be beam dup. He shrugged his eyebrows and shoulders at the same time.

How did he do that?

Maybe they were joined with some string. Maybe his shoelaces. Miles wondered if he was mental.

Eyebrows up, then shoulders up.

Updown.

Like a puppet.

And a Cadbury's mini egg in his throat went updown too.

Miles did the same in his seat on the tube. Eyebrows up, then shoulders up. It seemed quite easy and didn't interfere with his enjoyment of a Super Smash Brothers roundhouse combo he was unleashing on his foe.

He swung his legs with satisfaction.

After pondering his feet for a moment, the stranger looked up and addressed the worried carriage.

"I don't want your money or naffin', just wondered if I could 'ave a quick 'ug," he asked.

A ug.

That should be OK, Miles thought. Just no talking.

Without turning to face her, Miles dropped his Gameboy where he thought his mum's lap should be and with a shuffle, pushed himself out of his seat and towards the stranger who was taller than he looked.

Standing before him, Miles waited a moment for the stranger to bend down for the ug but he didn't, so Miles ugged his legs, little head turned sideways with a Chicago Bulls hat, ear against the train hum trapped like a fly inside the stranger's dirty trousers.

Come on, Faz thought desperately, shooting a glance at Salim. Hug me, man, then the others will follow suit. Your doing so will *legitimize* the act, yeah.

He was totally unprepared for what happened next.

For the little black boy wrapped in a head-to-toe puffa jacket (that made it a bit hard to walk properly) and innocent eyes that were unaware of the frozen concern in the carriage that was slowly thawing into action.

For Miles when he is real.

"Whaya do, ya good for nuttin' so-and-so?" a fuming woman yelled at Faz, snatching her boy away from his legs. "Gwan witcha!"

Miles looked up, mildly surprised to see his mum wobbling with fury like a washing machine on spin cycle. She swung her son behind her and began to hit Faz, who blinked and hiccupped with explanations under the blows, with a rolled up TV guide.

At Miles' feet lay the carcass of his Gameboy which had leaped out of his mother's lap like a frog as she rushed to his defence. The batteries had escaped and were rolling eagerly away from the hubbub into the next carriage like they had something fun to do.

A battery funfair to attend.

A battery party to throw.

Miles followed them with interest into the next carriage.

The washing machine didn't seem to be tiring of her assault on Faz, who was determined to give an account of himself.

"It's like an experiment, yeah. Breaking down barriers to, ooow, contact. You see if . . ."

I began the journey with a presentiment of doom that sat in my stomach, unfolding its scales like a pine cone, but I am starting to enjoy the spectacle of my best friend having the idealism throttled out of him.

And for a moment, a split second, I see just people in a carriage.

Before all sorts of judgments around race and the like, and how they're dressed, rush in to muddle things and get in the way of really seeing, seeing how like me they are with their anger and concern. Before assumptions, categories and pigeon-holes and the smugness of thinking *I know*, there's a pause, blink-of-an-eye stuff, really.

It's gone now but it felt like a way out of something. And now Emily comes to mind, her acceptance principally, and I wonder if I got it wrong somehow. It's strange, but I think something inside me has started to change, has softened. like ripening dates on a date palm.

The tube has come to a lurching halt at Seven Sisters.

"Come on, mate", I say, taking Faz by the arm and dragging him away from his comeuppance.

"Let's go."

Every Colour Under The Sun

Ursula Barnes

What follows is fiction and the characters are all from my imagination. However it is inspired by a real school and the real children, staff and parents in that school. I would like to dedicate this story to George Eliot Infant School and its wonderfully diverse community.

I

It's often harder for the parents, says Mrs Roy. The children are so busy, they haven't time to miss you.

You must be joking, I said. The first time in five years I've got a few hours to myself.

But she was right.

I cried when I got home. It was so bloody quiet.

I don't know what to do, now. I feel lost with Luce at school.

Get a life, Yvette says. Go to college. Make something of yourself.

She's my best mate, Yvette is. Kept me sane when Luce was a baby. Only she's moving soon, buying a place with Ricky in Hendon.

I'm not sure, I say.

She marches me along there anyway. Picks up one of their booklet things.

I might try hairdressing, I say. What do you think?

When you're with her, you feel as if you could do anything.

Afterwards Luce tells us she's made a friend, but she can't remember her name.

What colour is she?

I didn't look.

Of course you looked.

I can't remember then.

Me and Yvette are drinking coffee and trying to find out about school.

Think about it. Is she white like me or brown like Yvette?

Luce is stuffing crisps into her face as fast as she can.

She's green, the kid says.

Yvette laughs.

I told you they was weirdoes at that school. They let anyone in. They don't even ask what planet you're from.

And she starts making bleeping noises like an alien.

Yvette's a beautician. she does my eyebrows and my legs and everything. She's ambitious. She's taught me about that. Always wanted her own salon only now it's going to be both of us, just as soon as I've finished college.

I like the word *Academy*, she says. And *Finesse*.

I can see it. In gold on pink, with a pink and white striped awning.

She makes me fall about, does Yvette. We always have a laugh. Not that she understands about kids, not having any of her own.

Well, Luce's friend isn't green. She's black with a green coat, and she doesn't speak much English. Funny name. It turns out she lives on the estate too.

There's more black than white in the playground. Mums in headscarves and those long raincoat things. Not that I've got anything against it. Only you don't know what to say.

Yvette reckons we've got enough of them now. Time for someone else to take them.

There'll be more of them than us, she says. London should be for Londoners.

Who're you to talk? I say.

She's half Jamaican except she doesn't see it that way. Her dad pissed off before she got to see him so she kind of holds that against him.

They have a meeting for new parents. There's me and one other English mum and the rest you can't tell where they're from. An Asian man who looks more like a grandad. A little Arab sort of woman with a grey scarf on. One great big black woman has a baby slung round her in a cloth, sleeping. The council can take you to court if your kid's late for school, although that's only a last resort. I wish I had one of those slings when Luce was a baby. She never stopped crying. Neither of us did.

The green girl is definitely Luce's best friend. Why don't you play with Sammy, I say, or Kylie? I know their mums, it's easier. But no. It has to be this girl, Almaz, another one whose mother hardly speaks a word. A right bloody song and dance it is arranging for her to come to play. She and Luce dress up in my clothes and then I buy them sweets from the shop.

Luce and Almaz watch a video. They sit side by side on the sofa, Lucy's smooth blonde head next to Almaz's spiky black one. I think about hairdressing.

The moving date's been brought forward. Yvette's off on Monday. So this is our last weekend. Ricky's out putting in some overtime. We get a curry from the take-away and buy in some beers. We sit there, eating them on our laps, like we've done twenty times before, but this time it isn't the same. Normally she's just a bundle of laughs. Today she's quieter, like she's got something on her mind.

I wish you wasn't going, I say.

It's only up the road.

Not the same though, is it?

No.

I wonder who'll move in your place.

Could be some hunky bloke.

If only!

I'll miss you.

We clear away the curry stuff and wash the plates. Yvette rolls a spliff and we sit back.

I've signed up for the hairdressing.

You'll be great.

I dunno.

Take you out of yourself. Then when I've got the salon off the ground you'll be ready to join me.

Yeah.

It's hot in the flat so we open the double doors and let in the air. You can hear the TV from next door and the kids on their skateboards.

Then she says she's got a new product she wants me to try.

OK, I say, still thinking about the hairdressing and how good it will be working together. The course has already begun but I've only missed a few days.

The product is a new fake tan and I could do with a bit of colour.

I strip down to my bra and pants. My mum would have a fit, but Yvette's family never bothered. Yvette strips off too. She doesn't want to stain her jeans. It's bloody hot anyway. She has a gorgeous body. Sleek and brown as a chestnut. I want to hide myself. I feel like a pale photocopy next to her. Her thighs are polished wood. She doesn't even need a bra.

Luce is asleep in Yvette's bed.

I lie on a towel on the floor Yvette begins rubbing the fake tan in. She's got great hands. Big and strong, but gentle at the same time. She's very careful with it, that's her training. Her fingers are like water, trickling over you. She makes sure it's even so that there'll be no streaks or lines.

You'll be fine, she says.

This is her good-bye present to me.

When the fake tan has dried, we get dressed again.

We're talking about Luce, how she'll have to go home with a friend when we've got the salon up and running.

Where's she from, this green girl? Yvette asks.

Ethiopia.

Bob Geldof, she says. All starving.

I knew I'd heard it before.

Wasn't there a way?

Don't ask me.

I carry Luce home to bed. She seems heavier when she's asleep. When she's on her bed, I pull back the covers so that she's just got the sheet over her.

Love you, babe.

Love you, mummy.

She's got such a soft skin. No beautician can do that for you.

And that's it. Tomorrow Yvette will be gone and I start college. Everything will be different.

Going to college on Monday morning I have to pee about five times. It looks like a school from the outside, and inside's not much different. There are girls about the age I would've been if it hadn't been for Luce. They've got more sense.

It's a big room and, because they started already, they all know each other. As I walk in, everyone's chatting to someone else. They are sitting on stools at white benches, and a the back are sinks like in a proper hairdresser's and a shelf with bottles of shampoo and stuff. And a line of model heads with long synthetic hair. Some of the girls look at me.

Come in, says the tutor and finds my name on her register.

Find a space. You'll soon catch up.

I squeeze in between a Chinese-looking girl and an older woman.

We start off going over what they covered last week about hair types and shampoos. Then we move on to the pros and cons of rubber gloves and how to massage the scalp, the correct temperature for rinsing and how important it is not to get hair into the drains. And there I am at last, a student at college, taking my first steps towards a career and imagining all the laughs we'll have in our own hair and beauty salon. Tomorrow we'll start our first cut.

That wasn't too bad, was it? ask the tutor.

No, I say. Not too bad.

Luce wants to go to Almaz after school and I say she can.

Don't give her anything to eat, I say to the mother. She's got a delicate tummy.

When I pick her up, I get to look inside the flat. There's hardly any furniture and everything is tatty but it's all clean and tidy. Almaz's little sister is playing on the floor. Her hair is in tiny heated twists. I wonder if they teach you that at college. The mother's in the kitchen and there's a smell of cooking.

What is it, I ask?

She lifts the lid of the pan and shows me.

Lentil, she says proudly, as though she only just learnt the word. Onion. Chilli.

She gives me some to taste.

Ethiopian food, she says.

It's delicious.

When we get back, our flat seems cold and empty.

I want fish fingers says Luce.

Beans? I ask. Just give me five minutes, babe.

A few days later Almaz's mum and I leave the school playground together.

I'm going to college, I say, and the words make me feel good.

She's got the little one in the pushchair.
Yes, she says. I go to college also.
I wonder if she's understood.
I'm learning hairdressing, I say, ruffling up my hair.
I study English, she goes.
Oh, I say. That's a good idea.
Then she points at the little girl in the pushchair.
She college too. She crèche.
Almaz's mum speaks more English than I thought.

We walk to college together most days after that. The weather gets colder. School, college, it's all routine. I dream of Yvette and the salon. The tutor says I'm doing well, picking it up fast. Some of the girls are a bit immature. After college I walk back with Aster, that's her name. Her English is improving or I'm getting better at understanding or something. She is beautiful. She's sort of calm and there's this way she walks with a really straight back. I try to imitate her.
The girls sing this song from school:

My hair's brown and you hair's yellow
My eyes are brown and yours are blue
There's no one on earth that's quite like me
And no one that's quite like you

If you want to paint a picture of everyone
You need every colour under the sun.
If you want to paint a picture of everyone
You need every colour under the sun.

She brings me injera bread – the food they eat all the time in Ethiopia. I make her a Victoria sandwich. Most of the time she's on her own. She has a husband but he's away a lot. She says there's an Ethiopian church opening up somewhere. I say I don't like churches much. She's thinking of hairdressing too.

I haven't heard from Yvette for a couple of weeks so I ring her.

We've done it, she says. We've found the premises.

You can't have.

Didn't I tell you?

Of course she bloody didn't

Opening in two months.

Turns out she's in partnership with Jude – Ricky's sister. Only beauty, though. There's still opportunities for expansion into hair.

How's the hairdressing? she asks. How's my little Luce?

Everything's fine, I reply, but I feel let down.

I knew she was ahead of me, that she had to get started first, but I didn't expect it to be this soon. And Jude. I'm not at all sure about Jude.

We'll be having a launch party. You must come.

I ask if I can bring a friend. Yvette says sure, as long as she looks good. We leave the girls with another mate, and Aster and me catch the tube up to Hendon. She looks gorgeous, walking in that way of hers, a little sway, her back straight. She's wearing a green dress we picked up in the market. I'm in white trousers, halter top. Pity there was no one to do the fake tan.

It's a little shop, decorated in black and gold.

Finishing Touches, it's called. Beauty Consultants and Practitioners.

Inside there are flowers and people drinking champagne.

Hi, says Yvette.

It's lovely, I say.

We're pleased, she replies.

This is Aster.

Yvette gives her the once over.

I going to do hairdressing too, says Aster slowly and clearly.

Yeah, I add. We're thinking of getting our own salon – Afro and European in one place. We think there's a gap in the market.

The green girl! remembers Yvette.

And we all laugh.

II

Translated from the Albanian.

Day 1

We are in London. We are safe. I cry with relief and then remember what we have given for this safety. Everything. We have left all our belongings, our house, our friends, our country. I am cold all the time. The sky is grey.

The girl next door is ill again. She has fever and cannot sleep. Of course it is not just the fever that keeps her awake, but paracetamol we can give her. We are all exhausted and have run out of patience.

Day 2

Before we came I thought of London as I saw it on holiday when I was sixteen. The red buses, Big Ben, all the important-looking buildings, museums, the Thames. My feet were aching with walking round. My parents told me what a fine city it was and how lucky we were to see it. It is different now. We have not seen Big Ben this time. Just offices and shops and queues and the inside of this building full of refugees like us.

No one understands me when I speak and I do not understand them. I wonder why we spent all those hours studying English at school. Everyone seems to be from somewhere else.

Food is very expensive. We eat rice and potatoes.

Day 6

I am counting each day of this new life. I try to forget the past.

Today I found a school for Lorik. It is very near. The headmistress and the teacher seemed kind. They say there are other children from Kosovo in the school. He doesn't want to go. But it is the law. In any case, this room is too small for him. He can start tomorrow. It will be hard, but that is all the more reason to start soon.

"You will learn," I tell him. "It is easy when you're a child."

"Come with me, Mummy," he says.

"Of course I will, but then I will have to go. That is what happens in school."

I can imagine him standing on his own in the corner of the playground. It makes me cry a little. A lot of things make me cry.

I heard from my friend. Everyone has left the town now.

Day 7

Lorik went to school today. He cried when I left and his face was long when I picked him up. He would not speak to me.

Whenever I hear a radio or see a television it seems to be news of Kosovo and I am glad we are here. I am glad we are in London where it is safe and not surrounded by American bombs and murderous neighbours.

I felt the baby move for the first time. My child of exile.

Arsim is not supposed to work, but he is not used to staying at home.

Day 10

Lorik has a friend. He is not a refugee nor is he an English boy. Possibly he could be Indian. There are a lot of different nationalities. Lorik says they played at aeroplanes and bombs. Why couldn't it be cowboys or astronauts?

Perhaps I should be glad he is playing at all. The girl next door is still screaming at night.

Day 12
Lorik has learnt his first English. He says "Hello, Misroy." Misroy is the teacher's name.

He has been playing aeroplanes and bombs again.

"What happens in the game?" I ask.

"We get killed, of course."

A child of his age should not think these things.

They say he is fine at school. There is a special teacher to help with English.

I am proud of him. He is a survivor. We all are.

Day 15
I went to the hospital. Arsim game with me. We saw the baby for the first time.

They take blood pressure and do tests and then they gave me a scan. We could see very clearly: the heart beating, two legs, two arms, everything where it should be.

I hope I can have my baby in that hospital. She will be a Londoner. It is something to look forward to.

III

Ilse had always treated him on his birthday. He liked to be fussed over. She wouldn't let on until the day itself, then she'd surprise him. Lunch in a restaurant, a trip to the country. Once she'd taken him to the gardens at Biddulph. Once to Paris.

After she died, there was no one there to arrange a surprise.

"Sorry we can't make it." Stephen, the only son, had telephoned to apologize. "Joe's got clarinet. Come to us at the weekend."

"Birthday's don't matter at my age," Henry had said, but it wasn't true. For the first time in his life he was going to spend his birthday alone.

"I've nothing to look forward to," Henry had said.

It was the bereavement councillor who suggested the school.

"Plenty to look back on. It's fair enough at my time of life. Don't think I'm complaining."

The school, apparently, was always on the lookout for people to help in the classroom, to hear the children read, provide an extra pair of hands for the busy teacher. They were particularly keen on men.

Henry knew the school she meant. It was on a sprawling site, behind a high brick wall. The police were forever to be seen outside and the boys lurked in the streets at lunch times, bunches of yobs, looking for trouble.

"They're not local kids," he said, thinking of the neatly turned out school uniforms that left early each morning from his street. "No-one round here trusts those schools."

"I meant the infants," she said.

"I suppose I've nothing to lose," he replied.

Henry's St John's Wood flat was not one of the larger or fancier ones. But it had been a good choice. It had seen him through nearly fifty years of marriage – and more happiness than the start of his life might have led him to expect.

The flat was near enough to the shops, not far from the pleasant green of Primrose Hill, and there was a bus stop at the end of the street. Many times they'd caught the number 13 on their way to Selfridges or a concert at the Wigmore Hall.

"You'll have to move," said Stephen a few weeks after his mother's death.

Henry remained silent. He could think of no reason to stay except that it was his home. You didn't have to join the smart groups on their way to synagogue on a Saturday to find them reassuring. It was good to live among your own.

Stephen lived in Croydon, an area Henry considered soulless.

"But Dad, it's not going to work. You won't be able to manage on your own for ever."

The school was almost as near as the bus stop. Mrs Baker, the intense brown-eyed headteacher, offered to show him round the school.

"You'll be sitting on a fortune," he said. "Look at all this real estate."

"So many of the children don't have gardens," she said. "It's important for there to be some green."

In the playground a mass of multicoloured children swarmed around them.

"Hello, Lorik. Hello, Almaz. Hello, Lucy."

They stopped to pick up one with a grazed knee.

"Come on, Mohamed, let's get that cleaned up."

"Time drags," Henry explained. "At my age, you look for ways to fill the days."

"Don't overdo it. Even an hour or two a week would make a difference."

And he'd gone home full of it, looking forward to getting started.

"It's very community spirited," said Stephen. "But why not come and live with us? Then you can see your own grandchildren grow."

"They ran a police check," said Henry. 'It's all done properly.'

When Ilse had died suddenly, Henry, true to cliché, couldn't believe it. One day she was there, baking cheesecake. The next day she wasn't. Cheesecake was his favourite. He ate it piece by piece. She was younger than him. She was the energetic one. He hadn't expected to be the one to survive. After the funeral fuss had quietened, he waited for an official announcement to explain it had all been an error.

Class 1 was different from how he remembered school (the lines of desks, the stern teachers). Here the children chattered about their work without being hissed at to be quiet. He perched on a tiny chair ("That's a big one from Year 2," laughed Shamistra Roy, the class-teacher. "You get used to it.")

At the end of his first morning he felt dog-tired. He wanted to sink into a corner of the staffroom and fall asleep there. Perhaps he *had* overdone it a little. But his head was full of children's voices. The way they had crowded round him to show him their work. He had hardly thought of the past at all.

A painting of grandad in the rain.

A collection of misshapen letters which might (give or take) spell Abdullah.

A cut-out bear with cut-out clothes.

He tried to remember some of the names, but the faces and voices came more easily.

"I'll be here again tomorrow," he told Mrs Roy.

Henry knew they were lucky. Plenty like them weren't. They'd come to the relative safety of London as children (thanks to their family's money and foresight) and survived to adulthood. You don't need a past if you've got a future, someone had told him and Henry firmly believed this. He worked hard, kept his head down, made some money.

"Don't dwell on it," he advised Ilse. "What's done is done. Put your energies into Stephen."

He prided himself on his English accent. If someone asked where he was from he said St John's Wood. If they waited for more, he would explain that he'd grown up in Hendon. He didn't dwell on what had become of his parents. He never described himself as a refugee. He refused to have it mentioned.

And Ilse humoured him. They didn't talk about politics or religion or the time before they came to London.

"What's for dinner?" he'd ask.

"Any concerts at the weekend?"

"What are we doing on my birthday?"

She always had something up her sleeve.

Usually he worked it out. She'd have left some giveaway detail – a brochure, a cheque stub, a telephone number scribbled on the pad. He was a master detective, sniffing out clues – but he wouldn't let on.

"It *was* a surprise, wasn't it? You didn't guess?"

The birthday before she died it had been *Les Misérables.* Not that he was a great fan of musicals.

"That was a nice change," she said afterwards.

"I hope you didn't pay full price," he replied.

A present should never be something you'd get yourself; Ilse was adamant about that.

He got to know the children at at school.

Laura was sweet as pie with two little plaits, but her dad was in and out of prison. Fatimah's parents never spoke to her. Amy, seventh child of nine, could hardly look you in the eye. Sasha, the bright little Russian boy, couldn't sit still.

"Where do they all live?" he asked Mrs Roy.

"Locally," she replied. "The estates mainly."

"None of the kids on my street come here," he said.

"We're not good enough for them."

He read *Goldilocks and the Three Bears* to the whole class, holding the book up to show the pictures, just as she did, and doing the baby bear voice squeaky so that the children laughed and Lucy, said, "Do it again."

"They're exploiting you," said Stephen when he realized that Henry was there every morning. "That's a proper part-time job. You need to learn to say no."

"It's not like that," Henry explained. "I only go when I choose." But he chose to go every day.

Half-term was slow and lonely. Henry pottered in his flat and divided his thoughts between Ilse and the school children.

One quiet day he explored the council estate. He remembered it being built but he'd never ventured there before. Fancy being so near and never coming to see it! It had won architectural awards, he recalled.

Pale concrete glistened in the sun. He stepped round broken paving stones. He walked down one long terrace and was surrounded by familiar faces.

"Hello, Henry . . . Where are you going, Henry? . . . That's my flat over there, Henry . . ."

"Hello, you lot,' he said. 'See you Monday."

They went on a class trip to the zoo. Henry was given four children to look after. At lunchtime they sat on a bench and ate their sandwiches.

Abdullah said the lion was his favourite animal. Poor little Fatimah sat in silence, eyes like giant marbles. Kylie, always a handful, hid behind a fence, but left her feet peeping out so he wasn't worried. Chatterbox Sasha fell asleep leaning on Henry's arm.

Henry came home so tired he slept all night without waking once.

"You'll make yourself ill," said Stephen.

"I'm in the class photo," Henry replied. "Why don't you bring the boys over some time? I could take them down to the estate."

"My hearing lets me down," he mentioned to Mrs Roy. "Some of them are very quiet."

'Who in particular?'

He felt stupid for not realising.

"They're refugees," she said. "Only just arrived. They generally don't speak at all in the first year. Then suddenly in Year Two you'll hear them in the playground. That's the ones that stay locally. Others get moved on."

"Have you thought any more about the move?"' Stephen asked.

"I couldn't," Henry insisted. "I've got commitments."

Stephen, being bright, had got a place at a decent boy's school and, of course, Henry had made sure there was the money to pay. The boy grew up in a black blazer and grey flannels just like lots of other English boys.

"You're too narrow," he said to his parents. "All your friends are Jews."

He married an Irish woman, which was a pity.

"I'm going to be seventy-five next week," said Henry. They were talking about politics and pensions and special winter fuel allowances.

It came up naturally in the conversation.

"You're never!"

The queer teacher brought his coffee and sat down next to him.

"I'd not have put you a day over sixty."

At first Henry didn't like it. He had never known a gay man before. But then he thought, surely amongst all the men inn the office there must have been some. Kept it to themselves. You would, after all. What was that chap, Ray – the joker, full of the sort of things you weren't allowed to say now. Queer jokes, Irish jokes, Jew jokes. Sometimes he stopped before the punchline because he suddenly realized who was in the room. But not always.

This teacher was fine. The kids loved him.

When it was his grandson Michael's birthday Henry spent the weekend in Croydon. He joined the family at a bowling alley and afterwards for pizza. The boys squabbled in the car on the way home.

Sunday dragged. I wonder what it's like in Amy's house, he thought to himself. And what young Lorik is up to. He wished he was back with Class 1, sitting on a little chair, listening to their halting attempts to read.

"You'd be fine here," insisted Stephen. "Come down for your birthday. We'll do you a cake."

"Seventy-five candles," said Michael. "Wow!"

"Oh, and we've made a decision," said Stephen. "We're going to build a grandad flat. For when you're ready."

Every Friday was the birthday assembly. Today, after Mrs Baker had called out the birthday children for their song and their candles, the whole school sang her favourite song.

My hair's brown and your hair's yellow
My eyes are brown and yours are blue
There's no one on earth that's quite like me
And no one that's quite like you.

If you want to paint a picture of everyone
You need every colour under the sun
If you want to paint a picture of everyone
You need every colour under the sun.

"We have another very special birthday in school this week." Mrs Baker paused and looked round the hall.

The children twitched on their crossed legs.

"It isn't one of the children," she went on. "And it isn't one of the staff. Class 1, can you tell us who it is?"

A few pairs of eyes peeped in Henry's direction. Five children filed solemnly to the front and stood in a line.

Henry held his breath.

The school started up the familiar tune.

"Happy birthday to you."

Fatimah held up a large H.

"Happy birthday to you."

Sasha held up an E (wrong way at first).

"Happy birthday dear Henry."

Lucy held up an N and Lorik hesitated and then held up an R.

"Happy birthday to you."

Samer couldn't wait to hold up his Y.

If only Ilse could see this, thought Henry.

Afterwards there were cards and presents and a birthday cake in the classroom. The local paper sent a photographer and he posed with Class 1 crowded round him.

"Can you believe it? I'm going to be in the *Ham and High*," he told Stephen afterwards.

"It's only what you deserved," said Stephen. "After all the time you've given that school. You've saved them a fortune."

Henry imagined them all running round, playing together, working together, singing together. Every colour under the sun.

"I feel at home there."

The Black Russian

Ben Okri

The first time we failed but this time we will, we must, succeed in filming, in splendid Technicolor, our version of *Eugene Onegin*. There were four of us. We were going to use the local tools available. One of us had to be in the kitchen. There was a piece of rope that dangled from a projected bit of wood. When the train approached, at great speed, with its fires blazing, the one in the kitchen had to light the rope for it to catch fire as a sign to the train driver that he was to keep the train's fire blazing, to maintain his speed so that his fire and speed would fuel another scene where one of the women on a bicycle would ride forth, propelled by the speed, and then somewhere else another character would do what he was supposed to do.

It was all so well co-ordinated, and depended utterly on a one-take success, a once only event. It was then or never.

The rope burnt, the train driver saw it, the other dependent scenes went off perfectly, and as the train sped by one of us jumped on the open-backed platform where, to my surprise, I saw a black man who was an important worker on the luxury train. He was in charge of looking after the higher-ranking travellers. He was dressed beautifully, and had dark, almost blue, skin. And when I jumped on the back of his platform he smiled and said, "Welcome, Dubchyanka," and smiled again knowingly.

Whereupon I helped myself to one of his two freshly cut buttered sandwiches with a lovely slice of cheese on it. The one I chose had been bitten into by him, but I didn't seem to mind as I jumped off the slowing train. The black Russian jumped down too. He ran towards the local shops to buy some fish or caviar for the remaining cut of bread and to get a few more items for himself during the train's brief stop in town.

But someone else in our crew had jumped on his platform and had, in imitation of me, helped himself to the remaining slice of bread and cheese. I could see the black Russian's mild dismay and surprise as he watched this chap devour his sandwich. It was so funny.

Anyway, the scenes all went off well. The school teacher had her moment. Kuragin had his. The train was beautiful and was painted black. Colours were so perfect on that day. The women played their roles excellently. All the co-ordinated filming had been a great success, and we knew we had brought a great Russian classic home. It was the last day of filming. We did Pushkin proud, at last.

Magic and Mischief

Sandra Danby

The lift doors opened with a clatter but Elinor didn't get in. For the third time she checked her handbag. Keys. Purse. Cheque book. Paying-in book. Two dividend cheques to pay in, four bills to pay. She ticked the items off her mental checklist. Then she looked again at her keys. Had she locked the door? Oh dear.

The lift doors closed empty as she retraced her steps to her front door. Twinkle followed. She didn't need to tug once on the white Scottie's elegant Smythson pink leather lead; Twinkle went wherever Elinor went. And he knew her routines well.

Yes, her front door was locked. As her long fingers now bent with arthritis, struggled with the heavy bunch of keys, another fear popped unbidden into her head. The fire. Was it off?

A tall elegant woman, Elinor looked younger than her age. She was bored by other women of seventy-four who seemed pre-occupied with the twin domesticities of grandchildren and husband. Elinor, who had neither, had always been comfortable in her own company. She was satisfied with her own internal monologue and comfortably isolated herself from modern society. And she never sought the company of men. The thought of a strange man taking the place of her beloved Jack was unthinkable.

Within five minutes she pushed the lift button again and rubbed her aching knuckles. Door double-locked. Fire off. Windows shut against burglars (her apartment was on the third floor of a Georgian terrace). She ignored the nagging thought that she was getting a bit obsessive.

She humoured herself: it was simply her routine. Ever since the elderly man at apartment 2b had been found dead her routine had got longer. He'd died of carbon monoxide poisoning. The poor man lain there for six days before Mr Arif the newsagent called their caretaker about the uncollected newspapers for 72 Bentham Mansions, Whitaker Square, London W1. Since then Elinor made sure she spoke to the caretaker once a day so that if anything happened to her, he would miss her.

"Ping." Twinkle preceded his elderly owner into the lift on this, their monthly trip to the bank. Elinor told herself that everything she needed was in her little Mayfair square. There was the private garden in the middle where she could sit and enjoy the flowers, Mr Arif's corner shop for her newspaper and pint of milk, and the elegant Georgian square to walk around with Twinkle twice a day.

This was Elinor's world. After Jack had his operation their longing to explore further afield had evaporated. Having travelled the world in their youth, they were content to spend the autumn of their years in suspended animation in this small neighbourhood. They would spend the afternoon sitting on a bench in the garden; Elinor would read poetry while Jack read every word in the *Telegraph*.

Unlocking the garden gate with the heavy iron key never failed to lift Elinor's spirits. The garden was her oasis within the madness of London and it was rare to be interrupted by another visitor. She loved the simple restrained decoration and refined proportions of Robert Adam's classic square. She looked at her building, her eyes journeying upwards from the black iron railings, past the arched windows and fanlight over the door, to the triumphal arch flanked by tall circular Corinthian pillars. Much nicer, she thought, than Nash's Hanover Terrace.

Elinor felt a kinship with Robert Adam. He was a traveller too. He'd done the Grand Tour in 1754 and come back inspired. When Elinor and Jack had visited Rome ten years ago they'd recognized the grotesque decorations on the Vatican *Loggie* which Adam had recreated in Whitaker Square.

Elinor and Jack would sit in the garden and have a lively discussion about architecture. Elinor thought Adam a true romantic, soaking up everything he saw like a sponge. Jack thought him a bit of a tart who mixed sphinxes and griffins with altars and urns. Certainly in their square, Adam combined an eclectic mix of Etruscan and Pompeiian schemes which he had seen at the Herculaneum and Pompeii excavations with images from Estruscan vases. He must have seen those in the British Museum, Elinor mused. Adam's Grand Tour never reached Greece.

Elinor would sit on the bench, her hands tidily curled in her lap, and remember people she had loved, all now dead: Jack, the love of her life. Her sister, Belinda. Her parents. William, her son.

Since Jack's death, Elinor's world had shrunk to four hundred and fifty yards by seven hundred, the circumference of Whitaker Square. She ventured outside only once a month, to Coutts on the Strand, to 'handle her affairs'. The first Wednesday of every month at nine a.m. She'd never been able to shake off the fear, engendered in her gainful youth, of an interview with a forbidding bank manager. So she always dressed up.

Jack had always handled the money. And though she recognized her checklist as a delaying tactic to avoid leaving the flat, she also knew she had no choice. She'd run out of cheques and owed Mr Arif fifteen pounds. She didn't like owing money to anyone. It was against her creed.

"Ping." The lift doors opened on the ground floor and there stood Mr Bassett the caretaker, nervously smoothing Brylcreemed hair over his shiny scalp. He held the front door open and nodded slightly. "Your cab is here, Mrs Trentham. I couldn't get the usual people but I'm sure this minicab will be fine."

Elinor had driven a Mini Cooper in the sixties so found the idea inviting, though perhaps this minicab would be too low for her to get into. Her bones were a little stiffer now. She frowned upon any disruption to her routine. Mr Eliot from Elite Cabs always drove her on these monthly excursions. He understood her.

Standing on the step she looked for a Mini Cooper and saw instead a scruffy grey Toyota that had seen better times. A smiling black man held open the back door and beckoned towards her. Elinor appraised him closely. She noted his clean neaty-clipped fingernails and nodded to herself. Mind made up, she stepped forward. With a supporting hand under her elbow, the driver helped her into the back seat. He picked up Twinkle, placed him on the seat next to her and the little dog snuggled next to his owner who was comforted by his familiar panting warmth against her bony thigh.

Well, she thought, pushing aside her preconceptions about the driver. If he likes dogs he can't be all bad. Most cab drivers put Twinkle on the floor and some even refused to take him at all. But she was disappointed with the minicab, it didn't live up to its promise.

"To the Strand, yes?" the driver asked. Elinor nodded and laughed as if he'd said something funny, a default reaction when she was nervous. The car pulled into traffic and turned south onto Park Lane.

Elinor clutched the handbag on her lap and looped the handle through her arm to be safe from muggers. Jack had taught her well. What he hadn't had time to do before he died was teach her about money.

Not wanting to rely on her solicitor, Elinor had insisted she was capable of handling her own financial affairs. Everything had gone swimmingly except for one basic fact. She didn't know how much money she had or where it was. She knew it was a lot but was bamboozled by the money pages in the Sunday newspapers. Mini this and maxi that: skirt lengths as far as she was concerned. She'd refused all the bank's attempts to give her a plastic card. Almost twenty thick white envelopes sat in her desk drawer, unopened. An undefined fear of the bank's disapproval stopped Elinor from throwing them in the bin.

Out of the right hand window, Green Park gave way to the Ritz. Jack had often taken her tea dancing there in a wonderfully elegant room with high ceilings and a view of the park. They would dance to a string quartet and eat a tasteful afternoon tea served on rose-patterned china.

Elinor checked her handbag again. Yes, it was fastened securely. She always used the same handbag on these trips. Plain and scruffy so as not to draw attention to its contents, it was spacious enough to take the bundles of notes and still close safely with a satisfying click.

Sensing that the driver was watching her in his rear view mirror, she looked around the cab for his identification papers. Some sort of charm hung from the rear-view mirror, swaying every time the car turned a corner.

His picture was stuck to the dashboard. Peter Obende. Peter. One of the disciples. His parents must have been Christian. Obende sounded African.

Elinor loved Africa, she'd lived in Kenya with Jack for twenty years before coming back to London. Peter looked just like Solomon, their Kenyan houseboy. She'd been happiest in Kenya before Jack fell ill and they were forced to return to London.

Halted at traffic lights at Piccadilly Circus, she glanced at Eros. She'd loved and lost, but she'd lost out to death not another woman. Darling Jack.

The traffic cleared, the car sped down Haymarket and left into Trafalgar Square. Standing square in front of them was St Martin-in-the-Fields.

"That is my favourite church," said Peter. "My brother and I go there every Christmas to sing carols, it's on Radio Four, you know?"

Elinor did know. She'd sung there herself with Jack every year. But now she didn't go on her own.

"James Gibbs built it, it's his most famous church," she said. "Some people say he was Wren's successor but I think he deserves his own merit. He trained in Rome, that's why it looks a bit Italian." It was Elinor's favourite church too, another fine example of Georgian architecture. There were quite a few dotted around London. She'd visited most, with Jack.

A few minutes later, as they slowed to a half outside the ugly angular twentieth-century Coutts building on the Strand, Elinor wrenched her mind to the present.

"Thank you, Peter, for driving me today."

"I'll wait for you, Mrs Trentham, I'll take you home again."

He even sounded like Solomon. Elinor waited as Peter lifted Twinkle onto the pavement. Then she followed her eager dog into the concourse, stepped onto the escalator, and marvelled as she did every month at the real tree growing inside the glass atrium.

Twenty minutes later she emerged from the revolving door, evidently flustered and a little shaken by the speed at which the door spun. She sank into the back seat of the Toyota with a relieved sigh.

"Is something wrong, Mrs Trentham?" Elinor searched her pockets for her handkerchief to dab her eyes. It was made of fine white lawn, edged with lace and embroidered with her initials. She'd made it herself many years earlier, before the arthritis put a stop to her dressmaking. Now she played patience instead.

"Oh, Solomon. It's all so overwhelming. There's a new manager who doesn't know me. They speak so quickly and give me papers to sign. They don't understand that I just want to get my money and go home."

Silent for a few minutes to let her gather her wits together, Peter studied her carefully in the rear view mirror as he drove along Pall Mall.

"It's none of my business, but there has to be a better way of looking after your money," he said. "Coutts may be fine for the Queen but you need a bank that's around the corner."

"Well, I have always felt I'm rather a nuisance for them." Elinor laughed as if in appreciation of a joke, except it wasn't funny.

Peter smiled kindly at her. "You are their customer, not the other way round. You shouldn't feel a nuisance."

Elinor knew he was right. She often felt as if people humoured her because of her age, as if they thought she was sick or dotty. They spoke to her as if to a child. She was rather insulted by that. Solomon treated her like an equal.

"If you had a bank card you could get your cash and order a cheque book without having to go to the bank, you know."

Elinor thought of the envelopes in the drawer. "I think I've got a wallcash card but I don't know what to do with it. It rather frightens me. I know it's silly. Mr Arif has told me I can pay him by Visa if it's easier for me, but I don't want to apply to the embassy for a visa."

The Toyota turned right at the traffic lights into Whitaker Square and Elinor breathed a little easier at the sight of the familiar. "Here you are Mrs T, home." Peter turned off the engine and all three sat in companionable silence for a few minutes, the quiet broken only by Twinkle's occasional whine to be let out.

"What if . . .? No. Well, if you like I could . . ."

"What, Solomon?"

"Look, I know you don't know me and there's no reason for you to trust a minicab driver, but if you like I could help you with your cashcard. Find you the nearest cashpoint and show you how to use it. If you'd like, I mean. But if you don't want to, I quite understand."

Elinor smiled as she heard the embarrassment behind his hesitant offer.

"Oh, Solomon, that would be wonderful. Of course I trust you, after all we've known each other such a long time."

"Okay, Mrs T. But there's just one thing. I'm not Solomon, I'm Peter."

"I know, dear."

* * *

Later that afternoon the weather changed. It was the sort of rain that bounced up off the pavement and wet you in places that normally stayed dry. Donna moved her umbrella slightly to the right to stop the steady drip down the back of her neck.

Conscious of being fair and giving Christie equal shelter under her Liberty floral-print umbrella, she was forced to stand elbow-to-elbow with the woman she'd walked away from in anger yesterday. Donna felt uneasy about the physical contact and knew it was irrational. Perhaps it was guilt, pure and simple. Guilt. Because she longed to escape from Christie.

This was the third week of their European tour. Today, Wednesday, was their fourth day in London and they'd just come out of their second museum of the day. The tour was turning into a tourist treadmill, a tick-list of 'worthwhile things to see and do in Europe'. Surely the Grand Tour had not been like this.

They'd spent the morning at the Courtauld Institute and the Gilbert Collection at Somerset House. Then they'd drunk a cup of tea (dark brown and far too strong for their pallid tastes), eaten a tasteless couscous salad (just like the one they'd eaten yesterday at Stonehenge's Standing Stones café) and were now standing shoulder-to-shoulder on the Strand. Two middle-aged ladies dressed incongruously the same, like ten-year-old twins, in porridge-coloured raincoats and white trainers, they looked in vain for a black cab in the early afternoon rain.

Donna shuffled her feet and clapped her gloved hands in a vain attempt to generate some heat in her sodden limbs. Christie stood with her arms thrust deep in her coat pockets and didn't speak. On yesterday's coach tour to Stonehenge, they had started the day united in their hatred of unimaginative tourist traps and ended it sniping about irrelevancies. Donna had had one doubt before embarking on this trip to Europe. Christie could be very irritating. Her doubt had been proven. They'd dined separately last night and settled into an uneasy truce this morning.

Trying not to make eye contact with a seven-foot-tall black man in an ill-fitting suit who was leaning against a scruffy grey Toyota parked ten feet away, Donna waved vainly at an empty black cab speeding the other way without his light on.

"He's going home. He won't stop for you." He had an incredibly deep bass voice which reminded her of Paul Robeson singing 'Ol' Man River'. And he was as big as a house. Except he wasn't American.

"Where do you want to go?"

Donna assumed a look of deafness and hoped he'd take the hint. He didn't.

"Where do you want to go?" His voice was soft for such a large man. The power of his lungs stretched to full capacity in anger would be a sound to be avoided, Donna decided. His jacket, which was too small, was straining at the buttons. One will pop soon, she thought idly, if he doesn't undo it.

The next thing she knew they were sitting in the back seat of the Toyota, damp carrier bags around their ankles, heading past Bush House east round the Aldwych.

"Are you tourists? Where are you from?"

Donna thought quickly before she answered. Now they were in this mess, in a car with a strange black man driving off into the depths of a city they didn't know, should she make up something to hide their true identities? But what would that achieve? Determined to avoid upsetting Christie, who could panic for all fifty-two states, she pushed her own fear aside and told him they were American.

"American, ah." As he twisted to look at them over his shoulder, the lights turned green. A truck behind beeped its horn with typical London impatience.

"Would you like to see the sights?"

Christie groaned. "That's the problem. We've seen too many sights. We've been to all the attractions. They're boring."

Yes, thought Donna, they are. For once I agree with Christie. They do all the experience for you. We could leave our imaginations in the hotel because you certainly don't need it with all the multi-media presentations and interactive demonstrations. I don't want to see another audio-wand or listen to another plastic woman's voice. I don't want a list of facts and figures that don't mean anything. I want memories of real London.

"We want to see the real London." Christie unconsciously echoed Donna's thoughts and then stopped short when she saw the expression on her friend's face. Donna was wildly trying to work out where they were and was wondering if the best bet was to jump out of the car at the next set of lights. But all the lights were green and the car sailed forwards.

"I'll show you the Real London. I love London. Forty pounds, I'll show you London, misses. What do you want to see first, the multi-storey car park in Gerrard Street or the concourse at Waterloo Station?" He chuckled, a sound like the distant approach of thunder.

The two women missed the joke. They were too busy preening themselves at the 'miss'. It was some years since either had qualified for that description. But it was flattering all the same.

Christie patted her perfectly highlighted blonde hair.

Donna, who didn't want to go to Waterloo Station, wasn't thinking about her hair. She leant forward in her seat and said, "If you could just take us to our hotel, we really don't want . . ."

"Akemannstreet, this road was called Akemannstreet in Anglo-Saxon days. Did you know that? It went all the way from the Strand past Ludgate Hill."

"Your pronunciation of Anglo-Saxon is very good," said Christie. "Do you learn it in school here?" Donna raised her eyes in amazement at her friend's dimness. Christie's capacity for idiocy had surprised her on their first day at senior school together. And it still managed to shock her forty-six years later.

Unaware of Donna's internal monologue, the driver was now talking about food. It seemed it was a popular theme for street names during King Alfred's time. He pointed out of the window and waved his arm around. Donna noticed his hands, square and strong with neatly clipped fingernails. She looked up just in time to catch a glimpse of London Bridge – not the real one, of course, that was back home in America – and narrow winding streets straight out of the pages of Dickens.

"Fish Street Hill. Bread Street. Garlick Hill. And Pudding Lane, where the Great Fire of London started in . . ."

"No," said Donna firmly. "No dates. We won't come on your historical tour if you give us dates."

Christie nudged Donna and whispered, "Are we staying then?" Donna nodded. The driver observed the interaction in his rear-view mirror and smiled with satisfaction.

Realising that she'd stopped talking abruptly, and feeling, strangely, that she'd been rude to this giant man, Donna continued. "It's funny, I was fascinated by history at school and wanted to know all the dates when things happened. I memorized them. Andrew Jackson, seventeenth president, from 1865 to 1869. Came from North Carolina. Took office after Lincoln's assassination. He had two claims to fame. He bought Alaska in 1867, and he was impeached in 1868 for trying to get rid of his Secretary of War after a bust-up over the Civil Rights Act."

She hesitated, realising her tone sounded preachy. Christie was staring at her.

"Bet you didn't know that," Donna challenged. "But since we've been here we've learned about things that happened so many years earlier it makes America's history feel irrelevant."

"How do you know whose turn it is to go first when you drive up to a roundabout?" interrupted Christie. "I swear I'd drive the wrong way round." Ignoring her, the driver turned into a side street. Without a word, he got out of the car and left them.

Donna and Christie sat in silence and surveyed the scene around them. Closed shops with shuttered windows, covered with unreadable graffiti. Overflowing dustbins with a skinny dog tearing determinedly at a black bin bag. A flickering yellow streetlight gave the scene an eerie glow. Was this his Real London?

Nervous again, but not wanting to verbalize it and frighten Christie, and conscious of the tension between the two of them, Donna tried to work out what to do if things turned nasty. Goodness knows where they were, somewhere in the East End. She didn't fancy their chances going it alone. She looked at her *A-Z*. She always carried it to discourage taxi drivers from taking her on the 'scenic route' that involved passing Buckingham Palace three times from different directions. But she couldn't read the tiny type without her reading glasses, which were sitting on her bedside table in the hotel.

Not a soul walked along the road. The dog won its battle with the bin bag and triumphantly dragged away something unidentifiable. Nothing else happened.

Ten minutes later the driver reappeared, balancing three cups of takeaway tea. "For you. We can sit over there." He gestured towards a bench on a piece of waste ground next to a broken child's swing.

Obediently the two women followed him and waited while he dried the damp seat with his neatly pressed handkerchief. It never occurred to Christie to walk away. Donna knew this tour of Real London wasn't sensible, but she was at a loss how to get out of it without being rude to the driver. After all, he'd bought them a cup of tea.

He pointed to the wasteland. "One of the ways they found out about ancient London was by digging up places like this, you know," he said. "In olden days people threw things away in cesspits or rubbish pits or down wells. Near here they found bits of broken pots and beakers that were made in the Thames Valley. You know where that is?"

The women shook their heads and blew on their steaming tea. Too hot and too strong for their tastes, but they sipped it politely.

"It's forty miles from here. The pots were shelly ware, they knew that because there were shell fragments in the local clay. History – wonderful, isn't it? It brings London to life."

Feeling calmer than she had in the last twenty minutes, Donna swallowed the last drop of tea and wondered if it was going to be okay. The driver threw their empty cups into a litter bin and they drove on.

As they waited at traffic lights to turn right, Donna settled into her seat and realised they'd just passed up an opportunity to get away.

"You can turn right on a red you know, there's nothing coming," said Christie.

"I know you can turn right on a red light in the US, but we can't. It's not in the Highway Code. Although Ken might introduce it." He chuckled to himself, the joke lost on the two Americans. "He wants to charge us for driving into the city. He can cite the history books too. In olden days when ships used to dock here they had to pay a toll to the city. Sometimes it was money but they could also be asked for part of their cargo. At Christmas one German ship had to pay lengths of grey and brown cloth, ten pounds of paper, five packs of gloves and two saddle-kegs of vinegar."

"I can understand the gloves," added Donna, rubbing her hands together. "London in October is freezing, even if it has stopped raining. It never gets this cold in Florida."

"That's some shopping list," said Christie. "Perhaps grey was the new black that Christmas." The two women laughed at the shared joke.

"You ladies, you think you invented shopping. But men, we like clothes too. King James bought one hundred and eighty suits and two thousand pairs of gloves in five years. Five years. Fashion was big in the seventeenth century. Almost a quarter of Londoners had jobs in the fashion trade.

"Now we'll drive for a while, you can relax." The driver turned the radio on and the heater up. Lulled by the warmth, the ladies wiped the condensation from the inside of the windows and pointed out tourist attractions to each other.

"St Paul's."

"The Eye."

"Houses of Parliament."

"Albert Bridge."

Donna's eyes felt heavy but just before she surrendered to sleep, her bleary eyes focused on the driver's plastic pass stuck to the dashboard. His name was Peter Obende. His photograph didn't do him justice, it made him look like a convict in a Southern chain gang.

They dozed. Peter coughed reverently to wake them. The car was parked in front of B&Q at Wandsworth.

"There is the River Wandle," he waved a treetrunk-thick arm towards the council tip. Bemused, the two ladies watched a large green waste truck reverse into a narrow gap. There was no river in sight, not even the Thames.

"It's because of the river that Wandsworth became such an industrial centre in the nineteenth century."

"What sort of industry?" asked Donna.

"Calico works, match factories, dye works. It was the water, you see. It gave power to forty factories."

"You'd never know it." Donna turned 360 degrees and surveyed the three towering apartment blocks with their expensive shoebox river views, the jolly green Holiday Inn Express situated beside the bleak roundabout with what looked like entwined elephant tusks at its core. Elephants? Here?

Having circumnavigated the B&Q car park to the puzzlement of shoppers pushing laden trolleys, Peter turned back into the Wandsworth one-way system. No completely lost, Donna stopped trying to memorize street names.

"Where are we going now?"

"Merton."

Donna leafed through her red and blue Baedeker's guide to London. There wasn't an entry for Merton.

Twenty minutes later they pulled to a halt outside the Sleepeezee bed factory. Christie nudged Donna and pointed. Hung on the factory wall was a five-foot-high crest. The Royal Warrant.

"They made the bed Princess Di slept in." Peter spoke with pride and watched the wonder appear on the faces of the two middle-aged ladies. They stood in silence and looked at the unprepossessing grey building, oblivious to the steady stream of passing traffic behind them.

"William Morris printed his fabric in Merton. Liberty too." Peter gestured towards Donna's umbrella and she pulled her senses away from her memory.

Back in the car, the Americans fell asleep propped against each other. Emotionally spent and physically tired, they had no fear now of physical contact with each other, or of their driver. By 6pm they were safely deposited outside their Bloomsbury hotel.

"We knew a real Londoner would give us the best tour and we were right. Where in London were you born, Peter?" asked Christie.

"I live in New Cross." Peter pocketed their forty pounds. "You want a tour of West London tomorrow?" Without a glance to each other for agreement, the friends nodded.

* * *

Shelley rammed her hands further into her coat pockets and found a loose thread. Nervously she wiggled her fingers to enlarge a tear in the pocket lining. The clock above the jeweller opposite said it was 11.30pm.

"Oh, come on, Darren," she whined. She watched Darren walk towards the traffic lights three hundred yards away. She didn't see why they couldn't get the doorman at the Savoy to call them a cab.

As the freezing north wind whipped down the Strand, Shelley sought shelter from the wind-chill factor in the smelly doorway of an office block. Breathing through her mouth to avoid the smell, and careful where she stepped, Shelley gave vent to the frustration with Darren that had started to mount as soon as he was late to meet her from work. He should have booked a cab to take us home, she thought. You can't expect a black cab to want to go all the way to Barking on a cold Wednesday night. Stands to reason.

The play had been a mistake. She'd enjoyed it, she'd done it at school, but Darren had evidently been bored out of his brains. She sighed again, poked two fingers through the hole and reached her right hand inside the coat lining down towards the hem.

She wished he would make an effort and try to be a bit more cultured. She'd dressed up for the occasion. Little black dress from Warehouse, stockings and sparkly high heels. After all, you don't go to the theatre every night of the week, not like going to the dogs. She shivered. This cold wind crept into your bones.

Darren had insisted on wearing his blue fleece because it was warm. It may keep him warm but it made him look like a wind-blown rambler. And, thank you very much, that's not who she wanted to be seen with at *The Importance of Being Earnest* at the Savoy Theatre.

As Darren walked back towards her, shuffling his walking boots along the pavement, Shelley noticed for the first time a scruffy grey Toyota parked in the bus lane ten feet away.

With a feeling of detachment, as if she was observing someone else's experience, she watched a man climb out of the car and walk towards her. He was well over six feet tall, black, built like a rugby player and wearing a red football shirt underneath a too-small suit jacket.

"You want a cab?" he asked.

"No, tha . . ." Shelley's words drifted away on the biting northerly wind as Darren said "yes" and propelled her firmly onto the back seat.

"What are you doing, you idiot?" she hissed at him. "I am not getting into a strange car in the middle of the West End with a black man. Do you want us to be attacked?"

"Don't be stupid, it'll be fine. It's nearly midnight. There aren't any black cabs around, so it's either this or walk home."

Sitting in the back of the Toyota and wanting to be anywhere else, Shelley pressed her back into the seat hoping it might swallow her up. She crossed her arms and legs away from Darren to show him that she was angry. Darren didn't notice.

The car turned left off the Strand into a maze of streets beside the Savoy. Winding first to the left and then to the right, the driver turned into an underground car park and slowed the car to a crawl.

This wasn't the way to Barking. Shelley kicked Darren and scowled at him. He shrugged his shoulders helplessly and looked away. She could feel her pulse pounding in her stomach but tried to stem the rigor of panic flooding her face.

The car stopped. No one moved. No one spoke. The driver caught Shelley's eye in the rear-view mirror.

"One man, he was so nervous of me taking this shortcut he got out here and ran away. He left his woman. That's not right. A man should look after his woman." And he laughed, a huge guffaw straight from his belly. The laugh was friendly but the words, addressed at Darren, were threatening.

"I do look after her." As Darren held eye contact with the driver he reached for Shelley's hand, gave it a reassuring squeeze, and tucked it underneath his arm.

Calmer, Shelley looked at the driver and saw him watching her in the rear-view mirror. A minute later they were safely on Victoria Embankment, the river on their right, heading east. Darren watched the view as they passed first Blackfriars Bridge then Southwark and London bridges before turning left onto Gracechurch Street and wiggling through Aldgate to pick up Commercial Road.

Shelley monitored the driver's every move for signs of another deviation off-route. So far, so good. Just to be safe she memorized his name and photograph displayed clearly on the dashboard. Peter Obende. Mind you, knowing his name wouldn't do her much good if she ended up in bits at the bottom of the Thames.

She watched as block after block of shabby concrete flats passed by the window, past Stepney Eye Hospital and Limehouse DLR station, and she tried not to think about drugs. After all, if he'd wanted to rob them or kill them he could have done it back there in the car park.

No, perhaps he was a drug dealer. She gave up trying to decipher his torrent of words laced with an incomprehensible accent which she vaguely thought might be African. Darren didn't seem to have the same problem, though; the two men were chatting about football.

"Arsenal, Spurs, Chelsea. They buy foreign players because they're the best," said the driver.

"I think that's wrong. There should be a limit on the number of foreign players to give the local lads a chance. A lot of the London clubs have youth teams, you know, and the boys are bloody good. I support West Ham." Darren pronounced the statement as if it was self-explanatory, although Shelley knew that West Ham were propping up the bottom of the league table.

She watched Peter shake his head slowly in disagreement; the metronomic movement of the back of his head left and right had an hypnotic effect on her. The car heater was on high and the windows steamed up. She fought against the heaviness that dragged her eyelids down.

"I live near Millwall but they're rubbish, but sometimes I go to watch Charlton." Noticing the fogged-up windows, Peter turned the air vents on.

They were silent as the car swept through the Limehouse Link and onto Aspen Way, catching glimpses of the Dome, expensive apartment blocks, and motorboats moored in the docks.

The value of flats with a Dome view had doubled in the last couple of years. The prices were crazy but there were people crazy enough to pay them. Shelley sighed. She didn't approve of the Dome. The money could have been spent better, on other things for the locals. She'd refused to visit it, even though Darren had been quite keen.

As they turned into the Barking Road at Canning Town, past West Ham's ground, Shelley breathed more easily. She was on familiar territory. She liked going up west for a night out, but she was a home bird. An Essex girl and proud of it.

Even her name. She knew when Darren asked her out that they sounded like a kitsch windscreen sticker on a souped-up Ford Escort. But she'd still said yes.

Her eyes closed as she remembered why she'd fancied him. Two years now they'd been going out. A record for her – she'd never had a boyfriend longer than a year. Her mum was already planning the wedding, though Darren showed no sign of asking. Perhaps she'd ask him. She still fancied him, though sometimes those feelings were pushed aside by the daily art of survival.

"I'm a PC," said Peter suddenly, jolting her out of her reverie. "You know what a PC is?" A policeman, thought Shelley.

"I'm a pussy consultant." Darren looked blank. The words translated in Shelley's head and slowly came into focus like the swirling pattern in a child's kaleidoscope.

He's talking about sex, she thought, and, now wide awake, she panicked. Oh, God, why me? He's not a drug dealer, he's probably going to kill Darren and rape me. Please, Darren, do something. Her stomach knotted up and she sat ramrod straight, as if someone had pushed a bolt down the back of her dress. She shivered and pulled her coat across her knees.

Darren did nothing. Perhaps he hadn't heard him properly.

"He means he's a sex ther. . ."

"I realise that," snapped Darren impatiently.

Peter winked conspiratorially at Darren in the mirror and added, "I can tell you how to keep your woman happy."

"I don't need lessons on that, thank you; we do just fine," replied Darren, a little primly. Well, thought Shelley, that's not strictly true.

"You are a nice man. I will give you some tips on how to give your lady more pleasure. You know what I'm saying?"

Darren nodded and started to look interested.

"You can look at my website. www.pc.co.uk. But I tell you now for free. Normally this would cost you money, you understand?"

They both nodded.

"You take coriander and you rub it on the lady."

Darren looked stunned. Shelley burst out laughing. Was that what he was, a comedian?

"Where?" she asked. Darren frowned at her forwardness.

"Where what?"

"Where do you rub it?"

"You mix a little dried coriander with water and rub it on the lady's titties. It makes them very sensitive and is very nice. Don't put too much on, though, or it makes the titties sore. And never put it in the fanny. It's very painful."

Shelley giggled nervously, it sounded like an exfoliating treatment. "What about the fresh sort?"

"You know what fresh coriander looks like?"

Shelley nodded, thinking of Jamie Oliver's packets of fresh herbs in Sainsbury's.

Peter caught Darren's eye in the mirror and held his gaze without a trace of embarrassment. "You must eat it. Lots of it. It makes you hard for hours. You just keep going. Much cheaper than Viagra and you make your woman very, very happy."

"Stop here." Shelley pointed to a garage next to a Sainsbury's Local store. Repeating the instructions in her head like a mantra about what to do with dried and fresh coriander, she left the two men sitting in the minicab and rushed into the store.

Ten minutes later the cab stopped outside their maisonette opposite Loxford Park in Barking.

"Thanks, mate," said Darren.

Shelley waved goodbye to Peter as he drove away. What an experience. A PC who moonlights as a cab driver. So the advice cost Darren an extra fiver and the coriander was 89p. Cheap at the price.

She tapped her pocket and felt for the plastic sachet which had dropped through the lining into the hem of her coat. She kneaded the back of Darren's hand with the fleshy ball of her thumb.

They wouldn't get much sleep tonight.

The Christ of Crouch End

Tony Clelford

I am the Son of God. I am the Lamb of God.

Can't you tell? The whiteness, the spotlessness of innocence?

I am come to throw out moneylenders from the Blackstock Road pawn shop, cast out Pharisees from the Old Dairy. I am down from the mountain top, verily, even from the corner of Dickenson Road, to set my captives free. I am come to cast out devils from the customers of the Mind Charity Shop and the Stroud Green Joinery Company.

I will turn mortar into wine at the refurbishment of the White Lion of Mortimer, until all the builders are merry, even on a Monday morning. I'll buy olives from the Turkish greengrocer and the Italian deli, take two fishes from the Mauritian fishmongers and five loaves from Scotts, the Hungarian electric bakers. I will feed the multitudes at the Finsbury Park fun fair, putting Gianni's family out of business in the café, but fear not, blessed are the teasmakers, for they shall inherit the boating lake and all that lies in it. And everywhere I tread there will be fruitfulness. Hard avocados ripen as I pass the fruit and veg shops. The hot bonnet peppers in the Hummingbird supermarket will become sweet and juicy. Even the shops with no stock – the Ghanaian store that sells nothing but dusters, toilet rolls and chopsticks – shall be full.

Everton the postman, in his Rasta hat of many colours, foretold my coming, and at the Edgington Community Play Space a crowd will gather, waiting for me to emerge from the Piano Shippers. Cash 'n' Carry trolleys – lo, miracles, all their wheels will face the same direction – shall be pushed from the doors of M.A.H. Brothers, so styrofoam cups, paper plates and aluminium-foil serving dishes with reflective-backed lids can be issued to the masses. The field will throng with people, so many that not a speck of grass shall be seen, and I will preach from the commemorative bench. When I speak they will crawl forward to touch the hem of my garment, even picking at my shoelaces, and there will be miracles.

Visas to settle will be granted, plane tickets for emigration will arrive. Compensation for injuries at Hornsey Road Police Station or medical negligence at the health centre will be received. The infirm will dance without sticks back to the Tollington Park Day Care Centre. The colourful conga of pensioners in Bri-Nylon night-dresses and winceyette dressing gowns intertwines with traffic ignoring the sign saying No Right Turn into Stroud Green Road. Stroke victims regain control and tap out Latin rhythms on abandoned Zimmer frames, courier cyclists blow their whistles in unison and car horns will toot in support.

The infirm will lie on the muddy grass outside the Under Fives Pre-School Provision, and when I touch them they will rise and lo, another miracle, not a speck of dog turd will be stuck to their garments. Singing hosannas and 'We are the Champions', their voices will be amplified by speakers supplied by Sparks – reconditioned with a six-month guarantee, of course – rigged up by the previously deaf electrician from Sandilands.

The beggars outside Tesco's will throw their money back to the crowds and share their Special Brew with whoever is passing. George, the Independent Financial Adviser whose attic overlooks the traffic lights, will shout from the rooftop that endowment mortgages are A Bad Thing, before closing up shop and commencing a sponsored walk for Christian Aid and the abolition of Third World debt. The Continental Café, still awaiting the mammoth sheet of toughened glass to repair their vandalized window, will issue free ice creams through the gaping hole in their shopfront. Tenants from Tollington Court will tear up their rent books and from their balconies they will scatter the pieces of paper like petals, and when there is no more the florist will donate roses so my path can be strewn in red and pink.

Like Tannhauser's, my staff will blossom in the ungiving ground at the middle of the Tollington Park traffic lights, turning the junction immediately into a mini roundabout, where everyone gives way and all agree to go forward together in the same direction, in peace and harmony, even in rush hour. Blessed are the nearby estate agents, Malcolm, Jewish, and Christopher, Cypriot, for they shall inherit the freehold, even though their leases are on opposite sides of the road. As I pass the Turkish dry cleaners Mr. Brevet will say, "Never have I seen robes so clean before cleaning! Let me touch the hem of your garment; is it machine-washable nylon?" The Full Back pub shall be full once more, born again under the name of The Sir Walter Scott. Brazilians from the Universal Church of God at the Rainbow will convert universally to a God that does not believe in collecting money. The New Beacon bookshop, its poetry section untouched since 1979, will open its pages to me and publish my commandments in unlimited editions, printing them on thin strips of white paper to be threaded through the strands of the Afro hair extensions in the chemist's opposite. The rag trade sweatshops – wholesale, retail on Saturday only – will make a million white robes in high-fashion styles to distribute to my followers, throwing them from the first floor machine rooms. In the streets below, everyone becomes an angel. Oddments flutter, dove-like, from the windows and strew my path.

Each step of my progress takes me lower in man's estate, as I descend from the heights of Hornsey towards the depths of Arsenal. Outside the World's End pub I shall preach my sermon to the buses. The W3, the W6, even the lowly 210, shall stop and queue ahead of me. Like St. Francis, if the commuters will not listen I shall preach to the buses, to the Jamaican minicab firm and the British Transport Police squad cars. And lo, though they all keep their engines running, even when at rest, and the buses multiply behind them, yeah, the air under the bus station canopy shall still be fresh and clear. Power arcs down from the cracking wires of the Great Northern Electrics on the railway bridge and a voice from the police helicopter circling overhead megaphones through a gap in the clouds to say, "Yeah, truly, this is the son of God."

At the triangle by the station the traffic lights all turn red so the crowds can see my passing. The Mary Magdalens chewing gum just inside the Greek accountants' doorway will throw away their high heels and condoms to follow me, truly Seven Sisters in Christ. In the Blackstock News Agency, the Bengali woman at the till who cries when she hears voices trying to kill her will now hear silence and in it recognize peace and the way of the Lord here in Zone 2. A procession of four waiters from Il Cavaliere, holding a statue of the Madonna above their shoulders, will guide me to The Gunners Fish Bar and there I shall eat my last supper. The Arsenal 1st team and one substitute shall sit around me, my twelve disciples dressed in red and white, the colours of blood and Christ. I'll break bread and butter with them: this is my fish, these are my bones, this is the piece of cod.

Outside, the multitudes will stream towards the stadium, even from the distant plains of Corbyn Street and Dagmar Road, processing through the turnstiles of the North Bank stand until the terraces are full. The throng waits in silence; then, as I walk across the pitch, the underground rivers and the sub-turf irrigation system shall burst forth from the earth and fountains mark my path to the centre. There, at the heart of the circle, I will bless all of North London. The clouds will part, even the smoke from the London Borough of Islington refuse incinerator ceases, and I shall rise up to heaven as the referee's final whistle blows.

Biographical Notes

Ursula Barnes has worked as a copywriter, journalist and teacher and been a school governor for several schools. She started writing fiction at an evening class five years ago and is currently looking for a publisher for her first novel.

John Berger won the Booker Prize in 1972 with his novel *G.* His celebrated fiction includes *Pig Earth, To the Wedding* and *King.* His non-fiction includes *Ways of Seeing, Another Way of Telling* and *The Shape of a Pocket. Isabelle: A Life in Shots,* written with Nella Bielski, was published by Arcadia Books in 1998.

Charles Buchan is 25. He read English at Cambridge, and now works as a reader for Atlantic Books, an editor for Hesperus Press, and also for the literary agent, Laura Susijn.

Tony Clelford lived in Finsbury Park for twenty years. On the day before he left there he wrote "The Christ of Crouch End." He now lives on the edge of London trying to build a house while completing his first novel.

Sandra Danby is 41 years old and is Yorkshire born and bred. She has worked as a journalist for twenty years, editing magazines and websites and writing about interior design. Now living in Wimbledon, she writes short stories and is working on her first novel.

James Fellows trained as a teacher and has since worked learning from and occasionally teaching refugees. Originally from Birmingham he has travelled extensively in West Africa.

Maggie Gee has written eight novels, including *The Burning Book, Light Years, Lost Children* and *The Ice People*. Her last novel, *The White Family* (Saqi) was shortlisted for the 2002 Orange Prize for Fiction.

Toby Litt is the author of *Deadkidsongs, Corpsing, Exhibitionism* and the forthcoming *Finding Myself* (Hamish Hamilton, 2003). His books are published in the US by Marion Boyars. Toby Litt features in the Granta *Best of Young British Novelists 2003*.

Nick McDowell has been the Head of Literature at London Arts for three years. Before that he worked in publishing for ten years, first at Macmillan and Picador, then at Weidenfeld and Orion. He has reviewed for *The Times* and the *Financial Times*. He is the author of two novels, *The Wrong Girl* and *Four in the Morning*, both published by Sceptre.

Aydin Mehmet Ali was born in Cyprus and lives in London. She is the author of *Turkish Speaking Communities & Education – no delight* and the editor of *Turkish Cypriot Identity in Literature*. She has contributed to *Mother Tongues, Modern Poetry in Translation* (2001) and *Agenda*, and her short stories have recently appeared in *Crossing the Border*.

Efe Okogu was born in England in 1980 and raised in Nigeria and Vienna. He is a poet and writer who has performed widely in and around London and in Glasgow. Efe Okogu is currently a student at the University of North London.

Ben Okri won the Booker Prize in 1991 with his novel *The Famished Road*. His other books include *A Way of Being Free, Stars of the New Curfew, Astonishing the Gods* and *In Arcadia* (Weidenfeld & Nicolson, 2002)

Iain Sinclair's books include *Radon's Daughters, Liquid City* (together with Marc Atkins), *Lights Out for the Territory* and *London Orbital: A Walk Around the M25* (Granta, 2002). *Saddling the Rabbit* will be published by Etruscan Books in 2003.

A. Sivanandan is director of the Institute of Race Relations and editor of *Race & Class*. His fiction includes *When Memory Dies*, shortlisted for the Commonwealth Writers Prize and winner of the Sagittarius Prize, and *Where The Dance Is*, both published by Arcadia Books.

Fern Spitzer was born in Massachusetts and has lived in London since 1970. She has worked as a mathematician, artist, psychotherapist, day centre organizer and group work consultant, and is now writing a book of short stories.

Richard Tromans was born 1970 in Stafford. He has travelled widely and has worked in a number of countries. He now lives in London where he works as a journalist.